I0621521

Afterlife
in the
Higgs Field

By: Brian H. Cole, P.E.
2021/2022

Dedicated

Dedicated to my wife Patti Cole, who has helped

greatly with book content, encouragement, and

understanding.

Copyright

Registration Number: TXu 2-274-861
Effective Date of Registration: August 11, 2021
Registration Decision Date: September 2, 2021

All rights reserved. No part of this book may be reproduced in whole or in part (by any form or by any electronic or mechanical means, including information storage and retrieval systems, or transmitted in any form or by any means electronic, mechanical, photocopying, recording) without written permission, except by reviewers who may quote brief excerpts for book reviews (newspapers, magazines, electronic publications).

ISBN-13: 979-8987660904

Printed In the United States of America

Table of Contents

Introduction

This book starts with known physics and science and slowly steps into science fiction. This process is done to make the science fiction part of the book more believable.

Definitions of keywords are located in the back of this book for those that want more information.

Book Preview

It was a very sad time for Bret Zimberman. His parents were in their final years of life, and as with most people, Bret wondered what happens after death. The experiences of a person don't just stop, with nothing beyond. After all, why are we here anyway?

Bret reached out to religion and read about Christianity, Hinduism, Buddhism, and Sikhism. They are all wonderful religions with many similarities, but there was no hard link between religion and the afterlife, at least not for Bret. Religion can help, but you need to believe without hard proof, so this wasn't enough for him. Next, Bret turned to science and studied books on quantum physics in search of a link between our world (4-Space) and the next level that awaits us all. This research did turn up some weird stuff. For instance, we can affect quantum particles by simply realizing them, even at a distance, and this changes the particle from a wave-function into a particle. You may have heard of the wave-particle duality.

A few subjects of modern physics took Bret's interest more than others. These were Quantum Entanglement, Cooper-Pairs, and Super-Fluids, and these last two required super cold, near Zero Kelvin. The strangeness of this physics had Bret wondering…. Could there be a link between quantum strangeness and the afterlife? Zero Kelvin is where no heat exists, even at the quantum level. What is beyond zero Kelvin? What happens just above Zero Kelvin? Does Quantum Field Theory and the Higgs Field dissolve? He needed to experiment to see what could happen at these super cold temperatures.

Bret found that Cooper-Pairs and Super-Fluids both require temperatures near zero Kelvin. He bought a cryogenic-like machine and super-cooled a small chamber. Then Bret created a camera that he would place within this chamber. The camera, connected to his computer and monitor, showed what happened within the chamber of this super-cold environment.

He turned on the system and was witness to events never before seen by humans. Was he actually seeing back into the Higgs Field and seeing images of the afterlife?

Chapter 1: THE SCIENCE

WARNING TO READER: This first chapter describes some bizarreness with the current understanding of quantum particles. This science may not be interesting to many readers. If the science is not of interest, then the author suggests skipping this first chapter and understanding that Space, Time, and Mass have unknown and odd characteristics and that modern science does not know what is beyond the coldest possible temperature when even quantum particles stop vibrating and have no movement at all. Could this be an interface between our physical life and the Afterlife?

Current Day: It was a sad time for Bret Zimberman. His parents were in their final years of life, and he felt compelled to be near them when they needed him the most. As a result, Bret and his wife Barb moved 800 miles to be closer to them. Within six months, Bret lost both his mother and father, and it became clear that he had made the right choice to move closer. The deaths of his parents were an extremely difficult experience. It made him want to walk into a South Dakota Blizzard, but he knew things would feel better with time.

As with many people, Bret wondered what happens after death. He didn't believe that a person's experiences just stopped and were destroyed with nothing beyond. After all, why are we here anyway?

In his research for answers, Bret read many books on Christianity, Hinduism, Buddhism, and Sikhism. Bret also read books such as:

- Life Afterlife, by Raymond A. Moody Jr., M.D., published 1975 by MBB, Inc., and later published by Bantam Books, 1976, copyright 1975, 2001, 2015.

AND

- Closer to The Light, by Melvin Morse, M.D., published by Random House Publishing Group, Copyright 1990.

These books were helpful, but he wanted more of a scientific answer.

Bret started his career as an engineer, and science was at the core of his education. Fixing engineering problems is what he did, and an engineering solution was always there for problems with storm drainage, utilities, and the like. Still, death was unfixable, and where did they go after death? There had to be an answer that involved real physics and real science.

About 20 years earlier, Bret's wife (Barbara) had breast cancer. It was Stage 2, and options were available, including surgically removing the cancer, but with no guarantees.

Fortunately, the statistics of success were good. During this experience, Bret and Barb learned to differentiate what was in their power and what was not and then to concentrate on what they could control.

Barbara had the surgeries and chemo and was lucky to have successfully removed the cancer, but what a scare that was.

With much thought, Bret realized during this difficult time that life was truly for the experience. At least, that is what Bret believed. Being kind to others is also key, but the experience is what we are here for in our **3-Dimensional** world, **plus time**. For short, Bret called our physical world **3D+T or 4-space**, but the time component was the outlier, and in fact, in several advanced equations within physics, the time variable dropped out. How strange.

The experiments completed by physicists were astounding. It seemed that different results could be realized based on the type of experiment used. One experiment might show the quanta as a particle, but another experiment would show the quanta as a wave. During the last 100 years, physics has advanced to the very small level of the quanta, and some physicists would not count out smaller levels than the quanta as well. This disparity became the wave-particle duality and is still a question today.

The quantum world was much more complex and unknown than anyone expected. How can just seeing a photon or realizing a photon via experiment change the outcome? This question became a big disagreement between the great physicists of 1935.

Albert Einstein and two other physicists, Boris Podolsky, and Nathen Rosen, believed in causality and determinism. Still, Niels Bohr and Werner Heisenberg believed in what would be termed the Copenhagen Interpretation. The Copenhagen Interpretation basically says that we can't understand what we can't measure exactly and is, therefore, beyond our human understanding. Perhaps metaphysical? It's amazing that physicists were unsure whether the results were from Physics or Metaphysical.

Then there is what is called "Mass." Who can really define what "Mass" is without using an equation, such as the equation defining momentum? "Mass" is not the "Mass," we think we understand. It is not the hard surface we experience when we tap our fingers on a tabletop. What we are experiencing then is the repellant of charged particles, those from your finger away from those of the tabletop. The same charges repel each other (positive to positive or negative to negative).

Mass is really a super high frequency in which light can't penetrate, and "Mass" has components too. "Mass" is made up of "Rest Mass" and "Dressed Mass." Rest Mass is measured when at rest but never occurs in our 3D+T world, so it becomes a reasonable estimate, but to near exact numbers. Dressed Mass is developed due to the interaction of the quantum Mass particle (or fermion) and its force particle (or boson). For instance, an electron would interact with the force particle of the photon, creating Dressed Mass.

Another example is a fermion particle called a quark that has contact with its force particle called a gluon. I know that this sounds ridiculous, but it's true. Looking at Mass from this perspective, it becomes a much more mysterious, almost unreal.

Then there are virtual particles, which physicists know exist, but have never seen. They pop in and out of our 3D+T world by the zillions (or an infinite amount). They are needed for life to exist within our 3D+T. Clearly, something was happening within the quantum level that is beyond our understanding.

How does this all fit into the Afterlife?

Some subjects of modern physics took Bret's interest more than others. These were Quantum Entanglement, Cooper-Pairs, and Superfluids. Cooper-Pairs is where two mass-type particles, called fermions, combine to emulate a force particle, called a boson. Both Cooper Pairs and Superfluids occur near the temperature of Zero Kelvin.

It was this strangeness that had Bret wondering.... Could there be a link between quantum strangeness and the Afterlife? It seemed to Bret that there could be a link between our 3D+T environment and some kind of existence beyond physical . Zero Kelvin is where no heat exists, even at the quantum level. What is beyond zero Kelvin? What happens just above Zero Kelvin? Does Quantum Field Theory dissolve? Does the Higgs Field collapse just before it reaches zero Kelvin? Does this Higgs process reverse? If so, do our three dimensions fall apart into 2-dimensions or less, and what happens to the Time dimension? Bret understood that the Quantum Higgs Field is a field that turns quantum particles into three dimensions by slowing them down or adding what we manifest as Mass and also adding a time dimension. Bret had too many questions. A few experiments might answer some of them.

Bret's research showed that Cooper Pairs and Superfluids could only occur at temperatures near zero Kelvin. Fortunately, some experiments of this type do not require absolute zero Kelvin, but at a temperature he could realistically achieve, and this made him determined to follow through with his own experiments.

To achieve temperatures near zero Kelvin, Bret used what is called the helium-3/helium-4 Refrigeration Dilution technique. This technique could get temperatures below 1 degree Kelvin. He used pre-cooling in advance to make this possible.

SPECIAL REFERENCE: BASIC SUPER FLUIDS, by Tony Guénault, CRC Press, Taylor and Francis Group, Boca Raton, London, New York, 600 Broken Sound Parkway, NW, Suite 300, Boca Raton, Florida 33487-2742.

He planned to create a small camera based on materials that he knew were involved in Particle

Entanglement, Cooper-Pairs, and Superfluids, such that super cold temperatures would have low impact. The camera would be placed in or near a transparent container that could be cooled to near zero degrees, Kelvin. The camera would be connected to a standard computer. The electronic connection would be via large conductors (wires) to allow better transmission between the new camera and the standard components. The larger conductors were a precaution only.

The materials used were mainly made up of metals, but porcelain and other elements were also usable. Bret researched this fully and began the process of creating a very small camera that could withstand extremely low temperatures. He used several materials to complete five different cameras for testing. One of these must work.

Chapter 2: TESTING

Testing was the fun part. Bret set up a small transparent chamber for the cameras to see how they reacted to the extreme temperatures. Bret built several layers of boxes that were enclosed in vellum. The vellum created air pockets that would help insulate the super cold temperatures from the room temperature of Bret's computer. Still, he would eventually place an old cardboard box over this to maintain a comfortable temperature in his testing room (his home office). Bret bought a device on eBay (from Russia) that could produce extremely cold temperatures near zero Kelvin (using the methods explained earlier). He connected it to the transparent chamber and turned down the temperature, which eventually filled with extremely heavy mist and frost. He could feel the cold emulating from the chamber, filling the room with coldness. As entropy settled in the chamber, the cameras again came into view. All but one was damaged somehow, and one was destroyed (it blew completely apart). Fortunately, he had one camera left to test with his computer.

He connected the surviving camera with conductors and then to his computer at room temperature. Theoretically, the electrons should show some movement, even at super-low temperatures. This movement would create the needed electromagnetic field, and the energetic photons would travel down the outside of the conductor near the speed of light to Bret's computer.

Bret rigged the surviving camera outside the transparent chamber, with the lens barely within the multi-layer velum containers via an opening just large enough to take the lens. Even with a tight fit, the camera felt cold, but everything worked. Bret used a caliper to slowly move the lens within the chamber, and things began to change. What was going on? Could this be an interface between our physical world and the afterlife?

Bret knew a little about what is called Quantum Field Theory. In this theory, particles are made of fields. One of these fields is the Higgs Field, based on the Higgs Boson particle. As mentioned earlier, the Quantum Higgs Field is a field that turns quantum particles into three dimensions by slowing them down, adding what we manifest as mass, and also adding a time dimension.

The Higgs Field, also referred to by Brett as the Higgs Barrier, was very thin, so the lens adjustment was delicate.

Chapter 3: HOLY SHIT

The images were fuzzy at first. Frankly, Bret didn't know if anything was working at all. Then, something changed. It was subtle but distinct. It was like a cloud changing shape. Although this might sound like nothing, he saw beyond our 3D+T environment and somewhere within the Higgs Field, or Higgs Barrier. What the hell was this?

At this point, all Bret could do was watch, so he did, and he recorded the events as well, with no sound, just video, as he watched the cloud change shape many times on his computer's monitor.

The video eventually became clearer, and he could start making out somewhat familiar shapes. Then, after about an hour, Bret could see a familiar shape. **HOLY SHIT**, this was a human person floating in space, and it looked like the person was being advised by other human-like figures that were human-like in the face and upper body but were cloud-like otherwise. What was Bret seeing!!!!

Bret watched this group of human-like forms directing the fully shaped human in a direction away from the camera, and they all eventually disappeared into nothingness, or that was how it appeared to Bret. Is this an image or his imagination?

Shit! What just happened? The screen was still visible, but nothing more happened, so Bret shut the experiment down for the evening and he reviewed the recording multiple times. "**HOLY SHIT!**". That's the only thing that came out of Bret's mouth. This activity was all happening in his house, but in some other dimension or something beyond our 4-space environment, possibly in a quasi-mixed Higgs Field or something freakish like that.

Chapter 4: CONTACT

The contact came quickly after Bret turned on his unusual setup the following day. It was all so strange to see within the Higgs Barrier. At first, nothing happened. Bret waited until the computer and equipment warmed to full function, and then he saw some movement again.

The cloudy screen changed many times, with nothing else shown, but the cloudiness did show that something was happening. He watched for about an hour before something moved quickly past the screen. This movement was new, Bret realized. Another cloud person? Then it happened, and it was so fast it was instantaneous. A figure appeared on the screen. This Cloud-Like person said, "You can't be here; nobody has ever been here without dying first."

Bret said, "Wait,….. what the h…? I have to die to see this image?"

The Cloud Like figure said, "Let's get one thing straightened out first. My name is Miha. I'm an inter-physical interpreter that helps beings from the multi-dimensional physical world back into our home or to the Whole-One, where we were originally separated to go to a multi-dimensional space as a single entity in search of experiences. How did you get here?

Bret was breathless into silence. When he partially recuperated, he said he was a human person on a planet called "Earth," and that he experimented with a

Super-Cold, Super-Fluid environment to see past what he called the Quantum Higgs Field.

Some time passed in Bret's world (3D+T) before Miha replied, but time was only experienced by Bret, not Miha (communicating with Bret for his benefit). Miha said, "You are the first physical entity to get to this quasi-dimension without dying first. The words I use from now on are not perfect but are to be as best as can be described to you. Many physical entities enter here. Not all are human, but all are animal-like."

"Bret, you have entered a quasi-dimensional area never intended for anyone not transferring between the Whole-One and your multi-dimensional world. What you witnessed earlier was a person from your world of Earth, back to where we are Wholly-One. You saw our interpreters explaining what was happening to the newly passed person, and they then entered the Whole-One, where we all come from. Some call this Whole-One God, Allah, or any of many names, but we are with the original, the "One.""

"Bret, I hope you understand what I'm speaking. Please also know that my thoughts and understanding from you to me and from me to you are instantaneous. Your camera is for your visual only, and the images, such as clothing, are sometimes adjusted for your benefit. Also, your camera and screen pick up much more than what is in the 4-space of your room. You see what is happening in a much larger area, but nothing physical is needed for our communication, and all communication is understandable. It does not require interpretation. All types of animals communicate, but not necessarily by talking or sound. All are one with the Whole-One; communication is instantaneously translated into any communication or language. I will use Whole-One as the ultimate entity for your understanding as a Deity. Bret, I know you have already had communication with those that passed away and that you loved, including pets. Messages were transferred. You may have received them or thought that they were just coincidences. They were real. As a loved one goes thru the quasi-Higgs Field, they communicate, but because time is warped within this thin Higgs-Field or Higgs Barrier, the message is often delayed in your time. It does arrive, though, and it's up to the receiver to recognize it. Even pets communicate, but most people don't recognize the messages until they pass through the Higgs Field. Pets can communicate in a human language, but you already know this from the past, don't you?"

This communication was so astounding that it was exhausting. Bret said that he needed time to absorb this information, but before he took a break, he needed to know how to get ahold of Miha.   Miha said to call his name, and that was it. The communication ended, and the camera shut off automatically, and so did the cooling device. Bret knew then and there that he was not in control. He was just allowed to be a witness. Miha controlled the computer, the cooling device, and the camera now.

Bret fell fast asleep on the couch next to his

computer. He doesn't remember falling asleep because he was so exhausted from his new communication, but waking up, he did remember. The computer and cooling chamber was activated, and Miha said, "Hay!". Miha told Bret that he didn't want to startle and didn't mean to wake Bret up, but more communication was needed. At this point, Miha explained a little more of the quasi-Higgs Field. Miha said the Quasi-Higgs Field is an extremely narrow and unreliable barrier between the 3D+T world and the Whole-One. This barrier is a middle ground, where a little of both sides are real. For instance, a recently passed person on Earth could retain their shape within this quasi-world and transform from 3 dimensions instantaneously. Nothing could be depended on for sight, but some things appeared as they were in the 3D+T world, even the clothing a person had on or a collar from a pet.

Miha showed Bret an example. Miha had full control because he lived in this quasi-world his whole afterlife. Miha was talking to Bret close to the camera so that Bret could see every feature of his face. Then, Miha's face changed multiple times per second without notice but slowly enough for Bret to see the changes. Miha's face changed from man to woman, to dog, to cat, to some alien creature, then to a Sikh holy man, then a beautiful Asian woman. Then Miha stopped and said that he could go on with a trillion more, but Bret got the message that Miha was a spokesperson and controlled visual effects.

Then, Miha told Bret to ask questions to get the

"Wonder-of-things" out of the way so they could concentrate on the real questions of "Transformation of life through death, to the afterlife."

Miha was INSTRUCTED to continue this conversation with Bret, but Miha wasn't at liberty to say more. Miha knew what to do, though, even though Miha had never had this experience. Miha had lived many physical lives before, but none were so close between the 3D+T existence and the Whole-One. Never did these existences ever mingle...EVER.

Miha told Bret, "Life is not what you think. We are all the Whole-One. We, as a person, are not just a single and alone entity like you may have thought. There is only one Deity, but the one Deity incorporates all Souls from more places and times than you know." "It is impossible to describe to you less than 3-spacial dimensions plus time, or more than 3-spacial dimensions plus time, but that is unimportant now. You and your questions are what is important. You have somehow reached the entrance to the Whole-One, where no physical entity has ever reached before without dying first."

Miha said, "There was a character in your world that called himself "Einstein," and he came close to communicating with the Whole-One. He was a real crack-up, a funny guy. His thinking was so surprising with his thought experiments. These thought experiments worked well for him, and he did receive some recognition from universal thought. His first relativity theory was Special Relativity. It was easier for him because it included the Laplace Transform, a mathematical formula created years before Einstein, but General Relativity (his second relativity formula) was extremely difficult mathematically. It was about gravity and curved space-time. The human race has certainly made things fun for the Whole-One, but this new situation was (and is) completely unexpected. What a surprise to have a living entity communicating with us through what you call the Higgs Field."

Chapter 5: a **QUESTION,** a **SHOCK, and an ANSWER**

Needless to say, recent events blew Bret's beliefs out the window, except for the belief in one God. Bret was a deep believer in God, and during difficult times when he was younger and growing up, he called God his third parent. It was comforting to him because there was so much hate, yelling, and arguments in his younger years. Bret usually had good parents as long as they were not together.

Bret now sat behind his computer screen, numb and staring at a blank screen. This situation couldn't be real...........but it was real.

Bret needed to sleep badly. His sleep was deep, and his dreams were explicit. He dreamed he talked with an angel, could ask anything he wanted, and would actually get an answer. Bret had an extremely vivid flashback memory from 1958 in Denver, Colorado.

Bret clearly remembers a situation when he was about 2 or 3 years old. A clear image in his brain shows his father and his friend, a veteran from WWII, upset, and his father's veteran friend struggles with a stick, one end towards his head and the stick angled down, where his father's veteran friend tries to grab something at the bottom.

Bret slept for 14 hours straight.

When Bret awoke, he naturally had to go to the bathroom badly. After that, he knew what he needed to do. He had a specific question, and he called for Miha. Miha immediately responded, and Bret didn't hesitate. Bret asked to see his father's veteran friend (Mark). Miha could not see future events but knew something was different, so he didn't hesitate. Why should he? Time doesn't exist outside of 3D+T.

The next thing Bret realized was that an image of his father's veteran friend's face was on the screen, and communication was possible. Bret's father's veteran friend (Mark) started by saying that he appreciated knowing Bret and that Bret's father made a huge and positive difference in his life, but Bret broke in….."sir, I know you appreciate these things, but I have a question."

Mark stalled for a moment, indicating to Bret that he was indeed within the quasi-Higgs field where time somewhat exists, which was very real. Bret bluntly asked: "Why did you try to commit suicide in 1958 in Denver, Colorado? I was 2 or 3 years old, but I remember and know what happened….I was there with my father that day and had an eidetic memory of this event. The stick you held was a double-barrel shotgun. I see that clearly now. You were trying to get to the triggers, but you seemed clumsy at the time for some reason."

Suddenly the screen went blank. Then, out of nowhere, a face appeared, changing fast into different faces, just as Bret had experienced earlier. Then the face split into two, and both faces changed into different faces. This split continued until the entire screen was of 30 faces, changing continuously every micro-second. Miha controlled the computer, but Bret could still make out faces, and he saw faces that looked like they were from World War II, World War I, the Civil War, and past wars. He even suspected faces from the times of Napoleon and much earlier. What was more surprising was that he saw movement in the faces. They appeared alive, just as he was.

A strange and wonderfully pleasant voice then said, "You are wrong in what you are thinking. You don't understand at all. Since human life existed, wars have existed. Small wars were first, then bigger until they became tribal wars, then wars for land masses, then countries, then continents, and then planets, and with all of these wars, there is life-form tragedy with dead, wounded, and the horrific damage done to the innocent. What happened to your father's veteran friend happened to billions before him. He was, and is, human. World War II ended in 1945, but you must understand that human suffering from World War II did not end in 1945. In fact, the suffering continues in your time."

"Bret, a question….do you remember more from the time that your father's veteran friend had the wooden (assumed) stick?"

Bret, shocked as hell, stammered, but words came to his mouth…"Yes, I remember other neighbors having bad problems as I grew up in grade school.

Our next-door neighbor was a policeman and responded to a man in Denver that beat up his son badly enough to cause permanent life-changing damage. Another neighbor lady told my folks that if she showed signs of wanting a divorce, her husband would kill her. He was also a policeman working for the city and county of Denver. Then there was the talk amongst my friends of the bloody murder that occurred just a few houses from Denison Elementary School. We just joked about it, thinking it was not real, but it shocked me to hear that one of the police officers at the scene (and on the Denver news) had never seen so much blood all over the room. Also, one day after cub scouts, we dropped off one of my friends, but as we pulled up in the driveway, his mother came out the door running and screaming for help. His father was chasing after her, angry, and I think drunk from martinis. "

"My mother was new to driving in the very early 1960s. She didn't know what to do, so she got us out of there. At school the next day, it turned up that my friend and his mother and father were all okay."

Bret momentarily stopped talking. Then he said, "Well, that's a few things I remember." The voice then said, "Many situations that you've described were remnants of war-time aggression and emotional distress that was never dealt with properly, and alcohol made it much worse for many families." Miha then asked Bret, "What do you think now about your father's veteran friend, Mark?". Bret said without hesitation, "He was one of the best men I've ever known. He got his head straight and spent the remainder of his life helping other veterans."

The voice then said, "People make mistakes. In your current time, they have defined the acronym PTSD or Post Traumatic Stress Disorder, but after World War II (and all previous wars) they didn't know of this emotional & physical distress. It is real, and even though it was 13 years after World War II ended (in 1958), your father's veteran friend still had PTSD, and the martinis he drank didn't help at all. Unfortunately, billions of others also had PTSD, not just those who saw combat. PTSD is still not fully understood in your world. It includes a physical element that your doctors have not detected yet, but they will."

"Bret, your father's veteran friend, did the best he could, and what is important is that he didn't commit suicide. It was an unfortunate event that you did not need to witness. You must know, though, that thousands did follow through with suicide after WWII and all past wars, mainly in Germany. Although many Americans struggled for decades after World War II, many German soldiers could not face the 3D+T future."

"Just after the war ended, many captured German soldiers were just sent home. At first, it was wonderful, but soon it was realized that the Americans were looking for war criminals. For this reason, during the first years, the German soldiers defended their actions as following orders, and bring patriotic to their country. But after things settled down and years passed, many German soldiers had difficult times with what they did, particularly the SS. Suicides were daily occurrences during that time in Germany. How did they get caught up in the conspiracy theories and these Nazi lies? Could it have been from the radical German tabloid newspaper *Der Stürmer*?"

Bret was silent. Then he said, "WHO ARE YOU REALLY?"

Realizing Bret's true question, the voice said, "You are still talking to Miha, and I'm within the WHOLE-ONE. We are all ONE. Bret, you are talking with all of us from the past and to all of the universes… everyone, everyplace, and every creature from past to present, but the future is unknown, and causality and determinism (within physics) do exist."

Miha continued, "The quantum world is extremely different than the much larger biological scale of the world that you live in, but there are those within your world that have a better understanding of emotions and universal subjects such as physics. You might consider them as having Asperger's syndrome. Many individuals with this condition might experience life differently than you do, but they also have a better understanding of specific emotions and subject matter. Have you heard of the physicist Paul Dirac? He was the most significant mathematical physicist ever on planet Earth. He predicted the existence of **antimatter (the positron)** and shared the Nobel Prize with another well-known physicist of that time named Erwin Schrödinger. Remember Schrödinger's cat? Paul Dirac had many friends during his interesting life, each with a special endearing "Dirac" story, but you can read about him later. He ended up living in your country in Florida, working at Florida State University."

SPECIAL REFERENCE: THE STRANGEST MAN, The Hidden Life of Paul Dirac, Mystic *of the* Atom, by Graham Farmelo, Copyright 2009, hardcover first published in the United States in 2009 by Basic Books, A member of the Perseus Books Group. Published in Britain in 2009 by Faber and Faber Limited, the Paperback was first published in the United States in 2011 by Basic Books. Basic Books, 250 West 57th Street, 15th Floor, New York, NY 10107.

Bret said, "Stop …….just STOP, you are going too fast! Let me back up and ask again, Am I speaking to the Deity?"

Miha then broke in laughing. "Don't be so surprised, and calm down. I am One that once lived on Earth as you do now. My death brought me to the Whole-One where I am today."

"Your experience with Mark, your father's veteran friend, is understandable, and I can sense that you are starting to understand now. The human experience is singular, meaning that you are alone in yourselves.

This aloneness is critical for the experience. Without the loneliness, you could not experience things in your 3D+T, but know that many eventually return to the Whole-One. Everything is at peace with the Whole-One."

"The animal killed on the highway is now with the Whole-One. The child beaten to death by a drugged-up mother's boyfriend is now okay; the child is with us, the Whole-One, and is fine. Those that died in the holocaust are with us now and are doing great. The young black kid chased by KKK members and then tortured and hung for doing nothing wrong is with us now, and he is safe. The young lady that was killed by her ex-boyfriend, who said, "If I can't have you, then nobody will"...., she is with the Whole-One, and is fine. You get the point, don't you?"

Bret said, "Yes."

Miha then said, "All those that have passed could send messages of some type, but as mentioned earlier, it is up to the person in the 3D+T world to recognize the message. Many do recognize messages from loved ones."

"Incidentally, bad people also get messages, but most don't recognize messages very well because they don't expect them, but they do get them."

"Messages often come during the first month or so within what you call time, but they can be received for years after death. Most delays are due to the fluctuations between the 4-Space (3D+T) and the Whole-One. The depth of the Higgs Barrier constantly fluctuates, and the time dimension can change from what you experience to no-time instantaneously, but time can also fluctuate back. This fluctuation means that a message may be delayed. I think you understand. One more thing. Those that have passed through the Higgs Barrier can delay going to the Whole-One, or re-appear within the Higgs Field if they choose to temporarily not connect with the Whole-One."

"One example is from a young lady who was killed by her ex-boyfriend. She died, but her ex-boyfriend lived. The courts in your country didn't convict him. The killed young lady made it a point NOT to get past the Higgs Barrier right away. She would not have felt revenge if she had gone past the Higgs Field because only LOVE exists within the Whole-One. So she held herself back for some time. She wanted to cause frustration throughout the lifetime of her killer. She made him trip and fall down many times throughout his lifetime. It was always at the worst possible times. Once, he was at a job interview, where he had a physical test, handling sensitive equipment, but as soon as he grabbed the equipment, he fell over himself and smashed his head into the equipment as he fell. Needless to say, he didn't get the job."

"Another example she enjoyed was when her killer ex-boyfriend had a date. He was with his date at an expensive casino ordering expensive drinks. While he walked back to the table, carrying the drinks, he somehow fell on his face and broke the beautiful glass containers, but he just blamed it on the casino, so the casino made new drinks for free but watched him carefully. As he walked back to the table with the newly made drinks, he fell on his face again, but this time the casino had a video showing that her ex-boyfriend fell over his own feet. The casino kicked him out immediately, but his date stayed in the casino. She eventually won $5,427 on a slot machine, which is exactly what she owned in bills, car payments, and rent. How strange, right? During all of this, and more, the girl's ex-boyfriend never put together these happenings to his horrible mistreatment of her." Miha said that he never made it to the Whole-One, and wouldn't talk about where he ended up.

Miha went on and said, "Another example is with the black kid killed by the KKK. He went to the Whole-One immediately, but he briefly entered the Higgs Barrier at one point to direct reasonable justice on his killer KKK members, but he was smart in his request. He wanted slow and continuous justice, and he got it. The lives of the KKK killers were anything but comfortable. They lived for years but were tormented by alcoholism and drug addiction and were disrespected by most of the community that knew what happened, and the slam dunk was that the courts within your country finally caught up with them as they aged to death. Their final years were slow torture ending with horrible disgrace."

Miha told Bret, "If you're looking for further revenge-type examples, you will not be satisfied. I won't relay what happens in those situations, but I know that many dying people don't make it to the Higgs Field, and none of the KKK members made it. I don't discuss where they went."

Chapter 6: MANY LIVES, ONE SOUL

Miha told Bret of life and death through the ages.
Miha explained that these are true stories out of
trillions, and are told to help Bret better understand
the meaning of the cycle of the SOUL, from physical
birth in the 3D+T world, then life within the 3D+T,
then death, and then back to the Whole-One again. It
is the SOUL CYCLE.

Sub-Chapter 6A: Early Man - learns of compassion.

It was in the last Ice Age about 10,000 years ago. A
boy was born to a young couple within a tribe
consisting of 27 total members. The boy was named
Gak. He was the first child born in the last year.
Mortality during childbirth was extremely common
during this time, and it was also common that newly
born children would not survive the first year, but
Gak did live and was healthy. He was normal in
almost every way; except he had a little more
determination than most. Although it was getting
close to the end of this Ice Age, it was still very cold.
Ice was everywhere on the surface, but the ice gave
the tribe fresh, clean water. Below the iced-over lakes
was plenty of fish. The area in which they lived is
now considered part of Canada.

Gak Was lucky to have two good parents and good
members of this particular tribe that got along well
together. This tribe was large in those days. The
larger size made it easier for them because they were

not attacked as often by neighboring tribes. They were more feared by other local tribes. As a result, their life routine was to search for food, stay warm, and live the best life they could back in the ice age.

The 27 members of the tribe that Gak was born into had slightly more women than men. Most male tribal members paired with other female mates, except a few men with two female mates. Having more than one woman mate wasn't an ego thing; it was mainly for having offspring. All tribal members looked very similar, with dark brown hair and stocky bodies. The tribe was surviving their current Ice Age because past tribal members had created a base camp and had enough furs to keep the cold tolerable. Without the prior members of the tribe, they would surely have perished. It was the planning and logic of previous members of the tribe that helped with living in such a harsh environment. This tribe was living on the shoulders of the work completed by past tribal members.

Gak's tribe took a special interest in teaching their young how to hunt, fish, stay warm, and make spears and knives. The trades of the elders in the tribe were passed down to all the young tribe members, which amounted to three girls and two boys. Girls worked with the women of the tribe, preparing food and skinning animals. The boys were too young to hunt with the older men, so they gathered firewood and practiced their skills, slinging rocks and fashioning tools from rock and bone.

In the evening, the men would return with what they had caught, either fish or land animals. They would hang the catch-up for the next day to be skinned and used for food. The women and the men together started the fire. At about this time, all five children had some playtime. It was the best time of day for Gak, as he was the youngest of the five.

Gak doesn't remember much of his early years, but he does remember when he was about three. There were only four young people. One of the young girls was not there anymore, and he didn't know where she had gone. About this time, another child was born, a female, and she survived well. Gak doesn't remember very much about his younger years, but he did learn the language, which was simple. This tribe was small and didn't have much of a language. They had words for Important things, but most of their language was animated using sticks, drawing pictures in the sand or the dirt, and this is how the tribe communicated.

One day stood out in his young life. He was only about five years old at this point. The men had gone out to get some food during the day, and the women were carrying on their typical routines, but something unusual happened on this day. The men came home early. They ran out of breath, and they were scared. They talked about the Sabe. In their language, Sabe meant cats with large teeth. They talked about Sabe grabbing Gak's father. He put up a good fight but eventually, the Sabe drug Gak's father off. All the men tried to stop the Sabe from doing this, but there were other Sabes nearby as well. At one point, the men were completely surrounded by Sabes and had to retreat. They finally made it out safely, except for Gak's father. Gak was too young to understand what had happened, and he didn't understand why his father didn't come home that night. Everyone in the tribe was upset that night, but no more than his mother. Death was not uncommon for tribes of this time. However, the tribe had gone through a long time without any adult deaths.

After the death of his father, Gak didn't get playtime anymore. His mother was always busy, and she needed help all of the time. Some of the people in the tribe also helped, but they had their own lives to protect. Life was hard, and Gak grew up harder than most. During the next three years, Gak helped the women with cleaning and preparing food and particularly making the fire. He became very good at starting new fires and eventually became known as the Fire-Starter.

Gak grew up hard and fast, and all the tribes saw this. At eight years old, he was doing some things that adults did, including scouting for enemies. He lost his childhood and learned that survival was the ultimate, at least it was then, so he lived in the NOW, and the NOW is the hardest place to live in, given that the past is known and the future is undetermined. Living in the NOW does change a person's expectations and is very dangerous for others around him. He was ready for violent action at any moment, just as a dog or cat can be. Gak was a human animal, but with a different sense, a human sense.

The older boy of the children turned ten while Gak was eight. He was given a chance to go with the adults on a hunting trip. As the older adults and the 10-year-old child took off hunting, a female in the camp made a loud noise. It was Gak's mother. She walked over to Gak, then looked at the other men. She then pushed Gak towards them. She was communicating to the hunting team that she wanted Gak to go with them as well, even though he was not old enough for the hunting team, but she needed him to be a man and to bring in food. She was so tired from all the extra work she needed to do without her husband. The other adults seemed confused. They didn't know what she was doing at first, but then they understood, and they didn't like it at all. Now they have to teach two children to hunt. Hunting with simple tools and weapons was very dangerous, but they understood they needed to do this. Each family had to take care of their individual families and had little time to help someone else, so they needed to teach Gak hunting if they could.

The hunters were off, up and down the hills, crossing rivers, going to some of the best hunting grounds, where the land animals would be, and there were also good fishing areas. The two boys followed as best they could, but the slowest wasn't Gak; it was the 10-year-old. The 10-year-old had a harder time, but he stayed up with the adults reasonably well. At least Gak wasn't anymore a burden than the 10-year-old was.

The first couple weeks of hunting were hard for these boys, but they eventually became used to it. They learned how to hunt and fish, skin, and gut out the food to reduce the weight so that they could bring the meat back to camp.

Months passed, and the boys became good at hunting and fishing. Gak became closer friends with a 10-year-old boy and the other adults as well. They became a good hunting team and brought food back to the tribe. The food they killed was the smaller animals, not the kind that could attack them. The biggest was a small deer, but they saw the bigger animals in the distance. One was huge with long tusks, long hair, and a long trunk. Even the Sabe couldn't take these animals down. They witnessed the Sabe trying to kill one of the large animals, and the Sabe was trampled to death.

One day the entire hunting team was at a higher elevation, and they could oversee the whole valley. They saw several Sabe and a group of giant creatures with tusks and trunks. The large creatures didn't see the Sabes at first until one of the Sabes jumped on the back of one. The animal immediately reacted, knocking off the Sabe. The rest of the giant animals looked around to see what was going on and noticed the other Sabes. They didn't waste time, and they charged the Sabes. The Sabes backed off and left. It was an impressive thing to watch. Gak knew that his father was killed by one of the Sabes, and now he saw a giant creature that could take on the Sabe. If they could only take one of these giant creatures down, they would have food for months. At least, that was what Gak was thinking, to hopefully take down one of these giant creatures.

Gak became very good at hunting. He learned to anticipate the enemy and strike when the animal was weakest. He would watch them intently and watch their movements. He would watch them to see how they understood and observed the environment. He would become one with the animal that he would eventually kill. This insight worked well for him. Later, as he grew older, he became one of the better hunters in the tribe.

Photo (by author) taken at the Denver Museum of Nature and Science

Gak loved to hunt. He loved everything about it, from the search to the strategy to getting a clean kill and the dressing out of the animal. He didn't like to see suffering, though, and made every kill clean, or quick. If the kill wasn't clean, he would hurry up to make it clean. Of course, the food was the goal, but hunting was in his blood, as it was for all meat-eating animals, but it wasn't just land animals that he was good at killing.

Fishing was a little more trouble due to the ice, but he could sit for hours at a hole in the shallow, watching for a fish to come by for the bate he placed. Then with one skilled spear jab, he would secure a kill, and he loved to fish. He'd often eat the fish fresh from the water, but cooking it tasted better. It seemed that he was hungry all of the time, and this was the biggest motivator for him.

The tribe was successful in getting a lot of food. Each year they were a little better. Over the next ten years, they noticed that there was more standing water than before and more plants. With more plants, more deer and other animals would eat vegetation, which made hunting easier. The tribe became healthier and stronger.

In Gak's free time, he would watch the Sabe carefully and see how they hunted. Every time he saw the giant trunked animal take the Sabe down when attacked. Gak would watch intently at the actions taken by the larger creature. He was starting to dream of how to take this animal down. The other tribe members laughed at his dream and said he should forget it. That animal is too big, it'll kill him, but Gak still wondered, watched, and learned.

As the weather warmed, some areas became boggy and muddy. These muddy areas are the areas that the hunting team would avoid to get around and find easier food. The tribe had the same problems as the animals in the mud; it was more difficult to get around. They noticed these giant animals were even having a harder time and sometimes got stuck. That realization gave him an idea, and he knew how to kill the larger tusked animal.

Gak found the perfect spot, and he told the rest of his hunting tribe to chase the larger creatures toward this particular area. It was a muddy area on two sides, a lake on the other, and a dry area where they would chase it from, and that's exactly what they did. They chased five of these larger creatures toward this trap area. All but one got out to dryer land, but one was left in a boggy area and stuck in the mud. That's when Gak knew that he had it. The giant animal was terrified, but life was hard for them all.

Photo (by author) taken at the Denver Museum of Nature and Science

Watching this unfold was particularly horrible for the four larger creatures standing on dry land. The hunting team took their spears and surrounded the animal and kept it from coming onto the drier land. Then they would throw the spears at the animal to bring it down. This battle took hours, but finally, the creature went down, and Gak quickly put the animal out of its misery by thrusting his spear deep into the animal's big eye. They had done it. The other four giants eventually moved on.

Gak asked one hunting team member to return to camp and have the rest of the tribe return to them in the morning to clean the meat. The tribe back at home camp knew that the hunting team would not be coming back that night because they suspected that the hunting team would have too much work to do skinning after the hunt.

Night time approached, and Gak knew exactly what to do. He didn't want the Sabe to come in and take what they had just killed, and he knew that they would try, so as nighttime approached, he had fires on the dry side to protect their kill. He knew they wouldn't approach from the muddy or lake sides. Then they continued to skin the large animal. They were exhausted and set up camp for the night, and it became dark. The Stars came out, and it was wonderful to see the lights in the sky and to relax a little, but sometime during the early night, Gak heard rustling in the bushes. It was the Sabe, and Gak warned the other hunters. They grabbed their weapons and were prepared to fight to the death if needed.

One Sabe came in first, then was followed by others. The Sabe was a smart animal, testing for the best opportunity. They could smell the dead meat and were determined to have it.

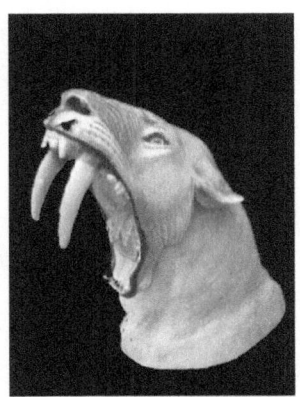

Photo (by author) taken at the Denver Museum of Nature and Science

As the night continued, it became a standoff. On one side was the Sabe, and the hunting team on the other. Gak watched intently as some of the Sabe attempted to jump but stopped short due to the fire, but Gak saw their intent. The other tribe members also saw this and became more frightened. They just wanted to make it through the night. Then they knew they would be OK.

The hunting team stayed up all night, and so did the Sabe. It was becoming morning, but it was still dark when Gak noticed the largest Sabe was getting more aggressive. It moved back and forth next to the fire, and its impatience showed Gak that something would happen. Gak quickly grabbed three of his best spears, and then it happened. The largest Sabe made a jump over the fire. The rest of the tribal members moved back, but not Gak; he moved forward, holding all three of his spears up to where he felt the Sabe would land. He was right. The Sabe landed directly on spearheads. The Sabe thrashed in pain and agony. Then Gak pushed the spears further into the Sabe. It didn't take much more until the Sabe went limp. The Sabe was dead.

The hunting team was in shock but elated. The team was screaming and yelling in happiness. Gak had killed a Sabe. The other Sabes on the other side of the fire appeared confused. They had seen their largest Sabe killed. Then they backed off as morning light approached.

After the Sabes had left, the hunting crew lay down and got some rest. It was still early morning when they heard the other tribal members coming down the hill. They heard screaming from the other tribe members. They could not believe the sight. One large creature dead, and a Sabe was killed as well, and all the hunting team survived. It was a joyous time. The entire tribe helped skin and clean both animals, and they spent days hauling meat up to their campsite. They would eventually prepare the meat with smoke to make it last longer.

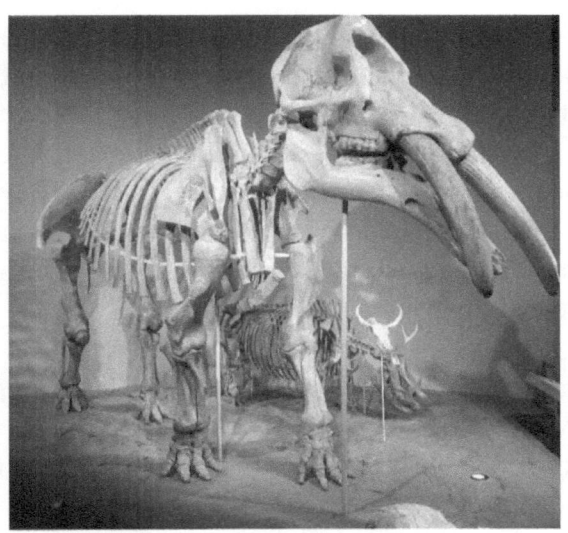

Photo (by author) taken at the Denver Museum of Nature and Science

It was his bravery that helped Gak gain status in the tribe. He was just a young man then, but he had done the impossible, and the tribe now had more than enough food for a long time. Things were good. The water was plentiful, and the weather was warmer. The ice was melting, and the plants were growing. Even the animals seem to be happier and more plentiful.

The tribe grew over the years. There were fewer deaths at birth, and the tribe grew in numbers. Eventually, Gak became the leader of the tribe and he made some of the hard decisions.

Life remained difficult with this tribe, but Gak still realized that if he gave special attention to those who needed help during certain times of their lives, they would grow up and add much more to the tribe. He spent extra time helping the young people. Now they all learned to cook, hunt, and clean the meat. They all learned to smoke the meat for preservation. They were united, and everybody in the tribe loved Gak. He was their leader, and he made the right decisions. He helped them survive and flourish.

Years went by, and the tribe flourished as a group. Now there were over 40 people in the tribe. The hunting crew went out daily to get more meat to feed the people. It was fun.

Another thing that this tribe enjoyed was in the evenings, on clear days, the tribe would all go out on a rock outcrop and watch the large light in the sky drop out of sight, bringing them into darkness and nighttime, and in the morning, they would often get up at the break of daylight, and watch this big light come back up, bringing in warmth for the day. The tribe liked looking at the sky both day and night. It was a calming time for them, a way to escape the harshness of their environment.

Gak was about 30 years old at this point and at the peak of his health. He led the hunting crew further and further away from camp, and they saw many wonderful things in different landscapes in different places. He decided to move the entire tribe further south to different hunting grounds. After weeks of food and water preparation, the tribe was on their way. They headed south to what is now the United States of America, more specifically, northern Michigan.

Travel was difficult, but they took breaks as they needed, and they found plenty of food and fish. Land animals and water were always available. The further south they went, they found fruit and flowers, and it appeared that life was getting easier the further south they went, so they continued.

Back in camp, Gak mated with a female that was a little younger than he was. She was born into the tribe next, shortly after he was born. Love is such a difficult term to use during this time. Survival was more of the correct term to use. Mating was a physical act, but caring for the offspring was done by both adults. Gak's life partner was named Ish. Gak felt strongly towards Ish, and he was extremely protective of her. He once nearly bashed another male's head in for trying to have sex with Ish. He loved coming home to her in the evenings, and nobody would get in his way in doing so. In fact, the other males in the tribe became a little frightened of Gak.

Gak and Ish had the best part of the skinned Wooly Mammoth (as we call this creature today). The best times for Gak were with Ish under the skinned Wooly Mammoth, and hunting, of course, and teaching the tribal members brought great satisfaction.

Ish was attractive, and she was strong and healthy as well. One time before she was with Gak, one of the other males tried to take her away from the group to mate, and Ish laid him flat on the ground with one side swoop of her fist. That male had the shock of his life and never tried anything like that again, but now Ish was happy to have a person like Gak as her life partner. She knew many others would like to have mated with her, but as soon as Gak showed interest, she never looked back.

Gak developed a lot of confidence in his abilities and started to show off. He took chances that he should not have taken. One time he took the entire tribe to an overlook that was just above the newest and best hunting grounds. Gak knew the limits of the Sabe, and he fully respected the trunked creatures, but Gak didn't know of all the dangers. While the tribe watched, Gak went into the valley below to make a kill of another animal they had come across, an elk or moose-like animal. To Gak, these were just larger deer. So, he approached the animal a little too close, thinking he could put it down with one blow of the spear. He placed the spear in a spot that he thought would quickly put the animal down, but that action only made the animal angry. It came at Gak full force and plowed Gak 20 feet in the air. Gak came down okay, but he was dazed. The animal didn't show any mercy because she had young nearby. Gak didn't know this and paid the price of a mother's revenge. In front of the entire tribe, Gak was trampled to death.

Gak's death ended the physical life of this Soul. It's not certain if this was the first life or a continuation of a previous Soul, but this was the first story that Miha told Bret. The Soul, during the life of Gak, learned empathy and compassion. The Soul entered the Higgs field. It would not emerge from the Whole-One until the time near Zero BC; see next.

Sub-Chapter 6B: Zero Year Man - learns of political factions, and of love.
Note: Within this book, except Early Man above, all years are AD (CE).
AD (Latin phrase for Anno Domini, meaning the year of the Lord starting with the first year of the life of Jesus Christ, starting with year 1AD) = CE (Common Era).
BC (before Christ starting with year 1BC) = BCE (before Common Era)

A peasant named Tasky lived in the Middle East, in what is now Israel. This area was considered the center of civilization at this time, at the approximate time that Jesus Christ lived.

The Soul of Gak had entered the human being of Tasky during late natal development, just before birth.

Tasky lived a normal childhood if there was considered such a thing as normal in those days. Religion occupied much more of the lives of the average person during this time compared with the modern day. Tasky grew up several miles from three small villages and was lucky to have his parents and one brother alive. They worked in a small area of land with crops and had a few animals, mainly chickens. Tasky had his normal chores helping out with the household, but he always had a chance to go fishing after completing his work. The fishing was always fun, and most of the time, Tasky would bring home a catch.

As farmers with animals, his family never had much time off except for fishing. His father (Franz) and his mother (Gali) were very good people and were raised as farmers their whole lives. In fact, their current lives were not much different than when they were younger. They were lucky to have lived in a quiet area near clean water and natural vegetation. The land was perfect for farming and produced good crops during normal rainfall.

Tasky's mother and father were neighbors and knew each other as young kids. They both grew up and lived their entire lives within a 10-mile radius.

One day Tasky and his brother (Vent) went down to the river as they often did, but this time they saw a large gathering at their best fishing spot. Someone was holding people in his arms and dunking them in the river.

Tasky's younger brother said, "Look. Those people are swimming with all their clothes on". This sight made Tasky and his brother laugh so hard they got stomach aches. This also looked ridiculous, but worse, they were scaring the fish at this fishing area. So Tasky and his brother went down to a different part of the river, where the water flowed faster.

Tasky threw out the fishing net, and he and his brother pulled it in. It was more difficult at this location than at the upstream location, but it would be okay for this fishing trip. They threw the net a second time, and it snagged on a rock, but they got it free and then pulled it in slowly. That worked, as they pulled in two good-sized fish. Tasky thought maybe this would be his favorite spot in the future.

Tasky and Vent continued to fish this spot. The net would occasionally get stuck, and they always got it free, but the main thing was that they were catching many fish. Tasky thought the faster water must be the key.

They had eight good-sized fish and had a great time through the early evening, but they wanted to catch just a few more before leaving. Tasky threw the net out further this time and was hopeful for another good fish. This time, the net caught on something, and Tasky couldn't free it. Vent said he would walk out in the shallow muddy water to help free the net. They both tugged. Then Vent said, "Tasky, we have a huge fish in the net. The fish is caught on a rock, but I think I can free it." Vent took one step, and he was gone. The place he stepped was deep, in the deep part of the river called the "thalweg ."Tasky screamed for help and started running down the river, hoping to see his brother, but he had no luck. He screamed for help, but who could hear? Maybe the people swimming and being dunked in the water?

Finally, after about 15 minutes, Tasky saw his brother on the shore, and a man in wild-looking cloth with a leather belt was pulling him out of the water. Tasky didn't recognize the man but was thankful for his rescue. Then Vent came around after a few minutes and coughed up water. After all the excitement and Vent drying out, their parents arrived, wondering where they were. The five of them were relieved at his recovery. This man then said he needed to return to his group before dark. The parents of Tasky & Vent offered some food to this man and asked his name. He turned down the food, said his name was John, and then walked away. Tasky, Vent, and their parents returned home and had a fantastic fish dinner with more fish to dry and salt for the coming days.

The years passed for Tasky and his family, and life was reasonable for them. Food and water were available, and they didn't feel any threat from neighbors. However, Tasky's father heard there was talk of trouble in the larger villages. Although they were not in any particular religious group, they did learn of three separate religious organizations, and each was getting louder.

These groups didn't necessarily have ties to the ruling government, but some were influenced, as you can imagine.

During this time, Tasky traveled to a nearby village to see if his family could trade goods. He took enough dried food to get him by for many days and enough water to easily get him from town to town. He was about 18 years old, and his parents fully believed in him. Although they were a close-niched family, his parents knew that he and their other son Vent would eventually leave to start their own lives. They also encouraged their son to be independent and follow his dreams. They always told him he was welcome on their farmstead as long as he wanted. That's how his father and mother started, by helping on the farmstead until they met each other, and then had their place nearby their parents. It was always good to have family around when tough jobs were too much for a married couple. This help included sharing food during difficult times or gathering crops when ripe during good years.

Tasky started his trip to the closest village and camped outside the farmed land. He knew the farmed land would be protected, so he ensured he didn't cause concern, which worked for him. The townspeople knew of his presence and were not threatened by him. In fact, some approached him to see what his intention was. He said he was looking for trading partners for his family farm. Many were very interested and wanted a different food source in drought years.

It was at this same time that the local priests approached his camp. They already knew his intentions and wanted to know more about his beliefs. Tasky simply told them he believed in God, which relaxed them. They then asked if he believed in Angels. Tasky didn't know much, if anything, about this, so the priest of this community started to explain. They told Tasky that the next level of life was an Angel, and many Angels are amongst them now. Some even take on human wives. This information shocked Tasky, but he kept an open ear and listened earnestly. When they left, he couldn't stop thinking of Angels. To think of another life beyond the life he was living was so surprising, but he found it comforting to think of his grandparents watching over him as angels, and he even looked forward to being an angel himself but was this real? He still had doubts. It was a good thought, though.

A few days went by, and Tasky had several interested in trading with his family, and the priests of the community were also happy to have talked with Tasky, so he went on to another village many miles away.

Tasky enjoyed the nights alone in the hills. He loved to see the many lights in the sky and always looked for those who decided to travel across the sky. It was mesmerizing, and he fell fast asleep each night, wondering what these lights were. Maybe they were angels, he thought.

The next village that Tasky came across was not as friendly. The town had problems with previous visitors, so outsiders were cautiously treated. Fortunately, Tasky had a way about him, and people warmed to him over the next few days. However, there was one similarity between this village to the last. That was that the priests came to visit him often to talk about life. The village priests here were different, though. They did not believe in Angels at all. They had a different perspective on God and the human struggle. Some things were similar to that last village, but others were dramatically different, and they did not speak kindly of the village that he was last at or another area nearby that had different views about God and the next level of life. Tasky was disappointed because he liked the angel idea but kept his feelings to himself. After all, these were new ideas to him, and he wanted to think of them more and even talk with his folks about them.

In any case, Tasky was successful in gaining other trading partners in this village too, so he moved on. Tasky had enough trading partners now, but he wanted to make one more stop at this third village first and then head on home.

Tasky had a couple of nights en route to the last village, which gave him time to think about things, and he also loved the dark night sky and the moon-filled sky. Either way, he loved being alone for a while. He felt himself starting to wonder what God was and what was the truth about humankind's existence. Were there angels or not? This trip was great for Tasky and opened his mind to different ideas.

The last village he visited seemed to be somewhat in the middle of his first two villages. This community was very hopeful of the future and was more trusting of him. The people were very similar to the other villages, and he did gain some additional trading partners. The priests here were middle roads from the other villages. They did believe in Angels, but not to the extent that the first village believed, but the stand-out thing about this village was that the priests believed in a savior. They said the savior was amongst them now and would improve their lives. This news was incredible to Tasky, and he could hardly believe this. He asked how the priests knew of this, and they talked about stories passed down from family to family. The written word was not common back then, but there was something called the scripture, but he didn't know what that was.

Tasky was happy with his experiences, newfound friends, and trading partners, so he went home. On his way home, he spent another night alone, but he had a nightmare about being killed by a large animal that trampled him to death. It was a nightmare, but it seemed so real. He woke up in a sweat, but he also woke up to an absolutely stunning night sky, and he prayed in the fashion of the belief his folks taught him. Tasky was completely satisfied but wanted a female companion and met someone from the last village. She was beautiful to him.

Tasky had many stories to tell when he arrived home, and his family was intensely interested in his experiences. Tasky listed all of the potential trading partners and from which village he met them. On a sheepskin, he sketched out a map of these villages in relation to his parent's home. The next step would be to grow and prepare trading foods, and other items, in which he could re-visit the villages and begin with his new trading partners.

Tasky also talked to his family about what the priests said at each village and how different their beliefs were. The two things he emphasized were the Angels and the Savior, but he was confused as to why there was so much difference between these three villages. His father (Franz) and his mother (Gali) both had stories of what they heard many years ago, but they were not as detailed as what Tasky was telling. Tasky's folks didn't know what to think of this news, but they also enjoyed the thought of a life after. It was just comforting, and both Franz and Gali did have dreams of past relatives from time to time. Gali even saw her mother shortly after she died. It was so real it was startling. This was a very interesting conversation for them, and Vent was all ears, but now they needed to plan for future trading partners.

Fortunately, the winter season was just ending, and the spring season was felt with warmer temperatures and more rainfall. His mother, father, and even his brother Vent were excited to start the growing season, hoping to make something extra in trades. Also, Vent wanted to see the wonderful things that his big brother had talked about. They all worked hard these next few months to clear more land for farming and traded for extra seed from nearby neighbors. They were enthusiastic about what Tasky had started, and even Franz wondered why he didn't think of this before. He was proud of his son for taking this initiative and would support this idea fully.

The family planted the seeds after any risk of cold weather, and they received rain shortly afterward.

It looked like another good year. Although droughts occur in this area, the last few years have been good. Even if they didn't sell their whole crop, they could start storage for more difficult years. Either way, this was a good idea to expand the farmstead.

The crops came up through the ground nicely even though they had some dry spells, but the family would haul water up from the river when they had these dry spells. It was hard work, but they were motivated and needed to keep the plants growing well.

About halfway through the summer growing season, Tasky surprised his family when he said he wanted to go camping alone for a few days. His family was a little disappointed because Tasky was always there and dependable. Still, growing older created changes, and Tasky's parents understood, so Tasky packed up and left for only three nights.

While Tasky was away, all that needed to be done with the crops was minor watering and a typical weeding. Most of the difficult work was done, and Tasky knew this before he left. He also filled all empty containers with water in case they had a dry spell.

Vent was older now and made his own day trips, such as down to the trusty fishing holes on the river. Fortunately, things went well for the family while Tasky was away, and things were also good for Tasky.

After three nights passed, Tasky returned, and he had wonderful news. He explained that during his first trip to find trading partners, he met a young lady he wanted to get to know better. All of the past few days, Tasky was visiting the third village (the one that believed in a savior). He met the young lady's family twice and even had dinner with them. He was allowed to take many walks with Avigal, the young lady's name, and he felt strongly about her during his short time with her. In fact, he asked her and her parents if he could marry her. This might sound strange to act so quickly, but it was normal back then compared to the longer pre-marriage relationships that we see today. In any case, he made arrangements for a formal marriage when his family traveled with him in order to make trades for fruit, vegetables, skins, etc. It was difficult for Tasky to leave Avigal, and this was a new feeling for him, but he knew that he'd be back soon enough. Along the way back home, he just couldn't get Avigal out of his mind. He felt that he wanted to be with her all of the time.

Tasky's family was as happy as can be with this news. They even had an outside feast that night and danced around an open fire until midnight. Then they all slept outside under a moonless night, with a million lights shining down on them, and shouted out when one of the lights crossed the sky. It was a wonderful night for them all. In the morning, they all got up early to watch the sunrise, and they knew it would be another warm day, so they started working on the crops again.

The growing season ended, and Tasky and his family traveled to all three villages. They sold most everything by the second village, but Tasky held back some of the best foods for his new relations.

Finally, they made it to the last village and made camp just outside of Avigal's home. Both families got along perfectly, and the language differences were minor.

The following day was memorable. The entire village showed up for the formal wedding, and final trades were made. Things couldn't have been better. After being married, Tasky and Avigal went up to the hills to be alone. They stayed there for two nights, where Tasky showed Avigal the beautiful night sky.

When they returned to the village, Tasky's family was ready to return home, and Tasky and Avigal went along with them. Their relationship prospered in the coming years, and they made many trips back and forth between their two families.

The lives of both Tasky and Avigal were greatly improved because of their close relationship. Everything seemed to be easier for them. They homesteaded on some land between their two families, which also helped trade with Avigal's village. They continued to trade with the other two villages as well, and Tasky and Avigal became successful. They built a nice home and had many crops and animals. They had so much that they hired Vent to help out.

Avigal's father worked with livestock back in his village and had access to mules and other larger animals. Tasky eventually traded for a couple of mules, and this helped him expand his plot of farmed ground. It was hard work, to be sure, but it was so worth it. The crops they produced helped the parents of both Tasky and Avigal as they grew older and couldn't work as hard. Everyone seemed to benefit. Even Vent was able to meet some of the local young ladies, thanks to being introduced by Avigal.

It was good that Vent was working with them at the farmstead. This extra help gave Tasky and Avigal a chance to go to the hills and camp and to look at the lights in the sky on dark nights with no moon. They did this every year at least once. They became as close a couple as can be.

Life wasn't always easy, though, and there were a few drought years over time, but the family learned to store food and cycle the food in storage to not lose any to rot, and during these drought years, Tasky and Avigal helped all those in need within the village as well as Tasky's parents. Working together was much better for everyone, particularly in hard times. Tasky and Avigal were well-regarded by all within this community and beyond.

Over the years, Tasky and Avigal had three children, two girls, and a boy. They raised the children as most did in the village that Avigal grew up in, but tensions grew between this village and the other villages, mainly on religion. It was more than just these three villages, though, as the entire region seemed to fall into three differing religions. What was worse, though, was the authoritarian government and the new taxes it was imposing on the small villages. This caused added stress between the villages.

The religious differences between the villages forced Tasky to search for new trading partners, so he left Avigal and Vent to tend the land and animals while he went to the larger town of Golgotha. He had never seen so many people before, and it was confusing as to who to talk to about trading. Unfortunately, nobody wanted anything to do with him, and he could sense danger in the town. Angry and frightened people were everywhere, so Tasky set up camp just outside of Golgotha in a rocky outcrop. That night he heard horrible sounds of anguish. He had no idea what was happening, so he decided to head back to his home the next morning.

He got up bright and early the next day and started his trip home, but something caught his eye. It was a large boulder near an opened cave, but Tasky didn't have time to investigate, and he was uneasy about what was happening in the town.

On his way home, he also came across another man walking away from town. He talked to this stranger and found him extremely interesting and knowledgeable, an amazing man. They talked for hours until their paths separated. This stranger knew a lot about religion and was very knowledgeable about the scriptures that Tasky had heard of years ago. At one point, Tasky noticed that this stranger seemed injured on several parts of his body, so Tasky offered to help this man with his wounds, but the stranger said he was okay and even felt wonderful. He said he was headed off to see many friends and that they would be surprised to see that he was fine. He even said that he was going there to heal them. Tasky thought this was very strange given the man's appearance. However, this man talked with extreme confidence and even authority. He said he was glad that the ordeal he had just gone through was over and that the future was bright. Tasky found this man so profoundly interesting, and he wanted to walk with him further, but their paths separated, and Tasky needed to get home.

They said good-by, and Tasky continued his way home. About a half hour later, Tasky heard the thunder of many horses coming his way, and they were traveling fast. He could see the dust from the animals. A few minutes later, several soldiers on horseback forced Tasky to stop. Tasky had nothing to hide, so he simply answered the questions as best he could. Unfortunately, they kept asking him if he had helped move a large boulder that was in front of a tomb. Tasky didn't see a tomb, but he explained that he saw a large boulder near an open cave. That answer just made them furious. Several got off their horses and approached Tasky in anger. One said, "Did you see anyone in the cave ."Tasky said "No" but explained that he had heard a lot of noise the night before as he was camping just over the ridge. The soldiers talked this over openly in front of Tasky, and he could see that they were frantic in their search for someone. They were getting angrier as time went on, and one soldier said, "We can't go back without knowing what happened to the tomb. They then turned back to Tasky and told him that he must tell them the truth and that they didn't believe his story. Tasky then became frightened about what was happening and why the soldiers were so angry. Then, the lead soldier held up his sword and, with one swift swoop, thrust the sword thru Tasky's body and through his heart. Tasky went to the Higgs Field before his body hit the dirt road. He didn't feel a thing.

Tasky entered the Whole-One immediately, and he was being guided by….Wait! Wasn't he just walking and talking to this man? Yes, and Tasky was just about to have every answer to any question he had. He couldn't believe the beauty as he was led through the Higgs Field, more beautiful than the night light in the sky.

Another life of this Soul had ended. The Soul, during the life of Tasky, learned of religious differences and the dangers of politics. The Soul of Tasky also learned of deep love for another person. The Soul fully entered the Higgs field and beyond. It would not emerge from the Whole-One until the year 1866 AD (CE).

That evening Avigal and Vent both saw a vision together. They both saw Tasky and another man behind him that they did not know. Tasky waved and said everything would be wonderful.

NOTE for clarity only: Vent stayed with Avigal and helped raise the three children and tend to the farm.

Sub-Chapter 6C: 1865 Year Man - learns more about compassion.

The earth's date was early 1865, just after the end of the Civil War. Three young men from the state of Missouri were returning to their farms near Springfield, Missouri.

During the war, Springfield was in the middle, between the North and the South. Before the war, these three young men didn't know much about the war because they were farm boys, and the news just didn't make it to their families very much, and when it did, they had other things they liked to do, like hunting and fishing.

The three men were Jonny, Will, and Bobby. Johnny was a little older and had common sense, even when things got bad. Will and Bobby were followers, but Bobby was the meanest. Not just from the war, he was always like that. Jonny and Will just put up with him because they were friends and had known each other for their entire lives.

As young men before the Civil War broke out, they got into the typical trouble of the time, stealing chickens and other food items. Still, all three of them were normal young men, hungry and looking for some kind of action, but there was one time that they got in trouble with the local law.

Bobby stole a horse from a nearby ranch just to have fun, and Jonny and Will were with him when he took the horse. He intended to bring it back that same day, but he ran that poor animal too fast, for too long. The horse was clearly in trouble when Bobby and the others brought it back to the ranch, and the local sheriff was waiting there for them. They eventually needed to put the animal down, which was extremely difficult for the owners. The sheriff required the three young men to make it up to the owners by helping out the ranch owners, and they did for a full year. It was during that year that they became good ranch hands and learned to ride well. It was this experience that helped them survive this difficult war. By the end of that year, the three young men had repaid the ranch owner for the loss of his horse.

In 1864 these three young men were all about the same age (16) when a southern officer coerced them into joining his group of fighters with new uniforms and nearly new muskets. What did they know about joining the fighters? Nothing, but they wanted excitement, and they knew hunting would be way better with these newer muskets. They said goodbye to their families and left with this southern group of soldiers.

Not everyone in this new confederate soldier squad had horses, so Jonny, Will, and Bobby walked. They walked for days. Along the way, someone said they were now in Tennessee. Neither Jonny, Will, nor Bobby had ever been out of the Missouri area, so this was kind of interesting to see other parts of the country. It was similar to Springfield but seemed to have more vegetation, and they knew more animals would be around, so they looked forward to using their new guns.

The group stopped for the night many times en route, giving them the chance to meet the rest of the group. The head officer was Sergeant Kirk, from the great state of Kentucky. He was given the unpleasant job of recruiting new soldiers to the Confederacy. He was a young man as well, at the age of 20. He joined the Confederacy in Kentucky when he was 18 years old and was a good soldier until he was injured. He broke bones in both feet when he jumped off a small cliff during a raid on a Union position. After that, he couldn't keep up with the regiment very well, even though he tried as best he could to walk. Fortunately for him, his commander saw that he had the gift of gab with other young men and thought he'd be better off recruiting new soldiers for the Confederacy. After his feet healed for a month, he was given a horse and two Corporals to accompany him out west to Missouri. They had a horse each, plus a wagon. They traveled to Missouri fast and started recruiting on their way back to Chattanooga, Tennessee, where he was to wait for news from his original regiment.

Along the way, Sergeant Kirk and the two corporals tried to train the new recruits as best they could. They knew that once they arrived at Chattanooga, Tennessee, these recruits would be picked up fast and sent to combat without additional training. Sergeant Kirk didn't have a stake in this, but he was the one that recruited them and had some sympathy for what they would be experiencing. As a result, along the route, he taught the recruits how to load and shoot the guns. He also helped a little with hand-to-hand combat suggestions. This mainly included knives; fortunately, all new recruits had their own knives.

The Great Smokey Mountains
Photo (by author) taken at the Denver Museum of
Nature and Science

The young men had fun with this training and got to
know one another as well, but they had no idea what
was coming up. For now, though, having this training
at their campsites was good. They even started to
think of themselves as a team of sorts.

Sergeant Kirk had recruited 14 men in total, including
the three from Springfield, Missouri. Each new
soldier was given a Confederate shirt and a used
musket. It was a long trip for Sergeant Kirk, and he
was glad to be only a day out of Chattanooga.
Unfortunately, that's when the trouble started. They
could hear gunfire just over the next ridge. One of the
Corporals went up to scout out the situation. When he
arrived back, he was white as a sheet. Just over the
ridge was a field of many Union soldiers, and they

were practicing with guns and other hand-to-hand combat.   But the worst thing was that the Union was this far South. What happened to the southern Regiment? When they left, the Confederacy occupied this area cleanly.

Just when they started to back off, they heard a gunshot behind them. When they looked around, they could see that Union soldiers surrounded them. They were captured, even before they could see battle, and they were taken deep inside the large Union Regiment.

This Union Regiment had seen a lot of battles, and the looks that these Union soldiers gave to the small group of Confederates told of hardship and hatred. They were also spat on and kicked as they traveled through this camp to an officer's tent by the name of Captain Clark. From there, they were processed and pushed into a small barn that was once used for animals. It stunk like shit, and that's what it was. Sargent Kirk was strong-willed through this ordeal, and the Corporals maintained as best they could. However, the rest of the recruits were confused and alarmed at the danger.

Captain Clark had become a ruthless officer on the Union side ever since his family was cut down in Virginia. He vowed to get even with those responsible, but it was impossible to know who made the killing. As a substitute, Clark was motivated to do as much harm to the Confederacy as possible. He took many chances early in his military career as a private and quickly moved up the ranks.

Higher-up commanders noticed his bravery and risks, and it took less than two years to get to the rank of Captain. Still, he was also smart and 100% dedicated, so he was made in charge of a Union Company. There were nine total Companies in this particular Regiment, which was over 957 soldiers strong. Out of the nine Company Officers, Captain Clark was the youngest and received his Captain rank last, so he got the grunt assignments, which included handling these prisoners.

Captain Clark didn't like this assignment and showed no mercy to the Confederate prisoners. Over the next couple weeks, the 14 Confederate prisoners were beaten and starved, and when Captain Clark had these soldiers out of sight from the Regiment, he tortured the poor men, and no one checked up on what Captain Clark was doing.

During this same period, the Union Regiment was on the move. They had small skirmishes along the way but nothing major, and every time the Regiment moved, Captain Clark became meaner and meaner. He saw the prisoners taking their time away from fighting the Confederate army.

Over the next few months, five prisoners died, including Sargent Kirk. His previous foot injuries had not healed properly, and without medical treatment, he became sick. Also, Captain Clark was especially cruel towards him because he was the ranking prisoner.

After six months, the prisoners amounted to 6, but fortunately, 3 were Jonny, Will, and Bobby. Given the treatment and the deaths of the other prisoners, as well as the upcoming winter, they had to make a move, or they knew they would die, and they knew that they had to make this move soon because they heard of a major battle upcoming.

That night, the remaining six prisoners waited until late at night, when most Union soldiers were sleeping. They previously noticed that the holding area that they were in was weakened by lack of maintenance, so in the early evening, they loosened two wall boards that would be wide enough to escape through. It was about 3:00 in the morning when they quietly knocked the two boards out and crawled past a sleeping guard. Sleep was hard to get on both sides, so when sleep did occur, it was often deep sleep. Anyway, they made it out to a deer trail and then walked until sunrise. They Made It!!! Or at least that was what they thought. It wasn't long before they could hear the Union Soldiers yelling, and clearly, they were being hunted. They knew that the Union soldiers would not take them alive, so they used every speck of energy they had to get further away, and they traveled south, hoping to run into other Confederate soldiers.

In about two hours, they stopped hearing anyone yelling. It was quiet when they walked into a small field of grass, and for the first time, they laid down to rest, and they all fell asleep.

They woke up to the sound of gunfire. It was nearby and coming from two different locations. They figured it was a confrontation between the Union regiment and some Confederate soldiers, and they were right; they were smack dab in the middle of the field between these two groups.

Fortunately, the grass was tall, and nobody noticed they were there. The battle had yet to begin, and there was just scattered gunfire. This situation allowed the six prisoner soldiers to crawl toward the Confederate side.

They crawled most of the way until they came across a plowed field. At this point, they would need to run diagonally across the plowed field to a thicket of bushes and trees near the Confederate line.

The Union and the Confederate armies were held up on wooded areas on either side of the open grassed and plowed field. Nobody saw the 6 Confederate soldiers crouched and ready to run across the dirt field. Jonny told the others to spread out to not give the Union Army a pack to aim at and to also zigzag, if possible, but to run diagonally towards the thicket.

After they rested a little, Jonny said, GO!!!

The six men stood up and started to run as fast as they could. Both the Union and Confederate sides were caught off guard, so gunfire stopped for a bit. Then Captain Clark noticed and commanded shooting at the six Confederate soldiers. At this time, the Confederate officers also recognized the situation. They commanded rolling platoon-type gunfire, meaning that the first line of soldiers would fire and then draw back to reload. Then the second line of soldiers would step up and fire, then a third, and then back to the first line.

Gunsmoke filled the air on both sides as the six Confederate prisoners ran for their lives. The Confederate side's cover was the best to be hoped for, as four Confederate prisoners made it to the thicket, but two did not. Of the four that made it was Jonny and Bobby.

Will and one other had been hit and were on the ground, but Will was the only one moving.

With all six Confederate prisoners either in the woods or on the ground, the gunfire stopped. At that moment, Jonny dashed back out to help Will, and the Confederate Officers said FIRE! The rolling gunfire started again, and the Union army now had a target.

Jonny fell to the ground next to Will. Will said he'd been shot in the leg but could run with help, so Jonny helped him up, and they limped the rest of the way to the thicket. They made it, and the Confederate soldiers went wild with excitement.

Just then, the Confederate officers said charge! And Calvary soldiers came out of the woods on either side of the field, surprising the Union soldiers.

It didn't take long for the Confederate soldiers to take control of the battlefield. The Union regiment retreated and reorganized back at their last camp.

Five of the Confederate prisoners were now free; one had died in the field trying to escape. All five were transported to Dalton, Georgia, where a medical facility was located. They were then sent to Atlanta, Georgia, for many months of recovery.

It was now 1865, and all five recovered. Jonny, Will, and Bobby requested to stay together when sent back to war, and they were reassigned to another Confederate regiment near Atlanta.

At this time, the Union army was moving solidly towards Atlanta, as this was a major transportation hub. Atlanta eventually fell to the Union, and the Confederate soldiers scattered and tried to reorganize, but the South was not doing good, and most soldiers just went home.

The war was basically over, so Jonny, Will, and Bobby traveled to the deep South for several months and even saw the ocean on the Gulf Coast. They loved the coastal waters and could not believe these warm waters at this time of year, winter. Was this heaven? Yes, it was the coastal area in the southern states of the United States of America. It was paradise. No cold, fishing all year long, and freshwater from rain, it could not get better than this, anywhere. They swam in these waters as locals looked on and thought they were crazy. Although the Gulf waters were not cold, they were nowhere near the nice warm waters in summer, so most locals didn't swim in winter, but these three men from Missouri saw these waters as warm, and they loved every bit of it. They drank their bourbon, ate good seafood, and enjoyed this pleasure they didn't even know existed.

Photo (by author) taken at the Denver Museum of Nature and Science

But most of the time, the joy of life had been sucked out of them. They were mostly dead inside. They found fun drinking with the bar ladies, but the Union soldiers would eventually make it down to every southern location, and the three young men stayed away from them. They traveled west, following the Gulf of Mexico, and partied all along the way, eventually making it to New Orleans. This city was broken-down and filled with injured Confederate soldiers in need and many Union soldiers patrolling the streets day and night.   The three men stayed for a while and were held up at a place called Elsie's in what is called the French Quarter. It was fun there, and each guy had one special lady to have fun with exclusively. Elsie also had a bathhouse on the first level, which was amazing. These guys hadn't been clean in…well, months since being in the hospital in Atlanta. The three men spent much of their money on these ladies, booze, and the hot bath house. They also loved the food, with critters they had never heard of, like shrimp and other fish they didn't have back in Missouri. It was a party every night for weeks, but they eventually knew they should be on their way home before someone did something stupid, like Bobby.

Photo (by author) taken at the Denver Museum of Nature and Science

While drinking too much bourbon one evening, Jonny looked at Will and said, "We should go home." Will looked down at his drink, looked Jonny straight in the eyes, and agreed. They then both looked over at Bobby, having fun with his girl, and said to each other, we'll talk with him tomorrow. Then the next day, they headed out. The girls were getting to like these fellas, but they had other clients too, so they reluctantly said goodbye but followed that with "Come on back anytime."

The three men headed up the Mississippi River and camped on its banks for many nights. Catfish were plentiful, and some locals helped them as well with bread and vegetables, but everybody was hurting after this horrific war. If help was needed, these men would also help out for a day or two, particularly if the locals were older or had injuries in the household. Injured people were everywhere they went, and these men knew that most wouldn't survive the next year or so. Life was difficult, even for the healthy.

The three men watched the Union boats traveling down the river, and they started to miss their families more than ever and wondered how they were doing during the wartime. They were typically more responsible, but the booze seemed to take that away, and while they were traveling, they didn't carry booze, so they detoxified along the route. It was a little difficult at first, but after a couple of days, they regained their strength and senses.

They didn't really know which way to go to get

home, so they continued up the Mississippi until they got to New Madrid, Missouri. They knew about New Madrid because they had gone through New Madrid as new recruits. It was enjoyable to see this place again, and they remembered the excitement they had in seeing it for the first time, but it was also sad to think of the last time they were there and all of the crap and torture they had to endure since then. They were so young and innocent then, but now they knew their way home, and it was exciting to think of being home again.

War was hell for them and everyone else, but all three made it through the war together, and that was a miracle. Unfortunately, they all lost their youthful spirits and became hardened men of 17 years old. They learned to curse profusely, to drink Kentucky and Tennessee Bourbon, and they liked it a lot…too much. It temporarily made up for the horrors they had just experienced, and during the war, they all visited those government-sponsored lady tents more than a lot of times. They all had early states of syphilis from either these tents or Elsie's place; they just didn't know they had it at this time.

They didn't mind taking some crops from local farms as they traveled back to their farms. Although they grew up as good kids, the war changed everything for them, so stealing wasn't a big deal, as they did that as kids as well, but they also helped out others that needed help, and help was needed everywhere. The time at war changed them for the worse, much worse, but finally, they made it home to their parents and other siblings that never left for war.

When the young men each approached their home farmsteads, they were greeted with extreme love and happiness. All of the families never thought they'd see them again. However, the families immediately saw the differences in these 17-year-old men and took them in as though they had never left. Perhaps they could nurse the horribleness of the war out of them.

The city of Springfield had several homecoming parties for all the soldiers, but these parties were stifled because the soldiers coming home were both from the North and the South. Anger boiled over several times, and fist fights were common. After all, Springfield was a good-sized city, even back in those days, so they saw many soldiers from both sides of this war.

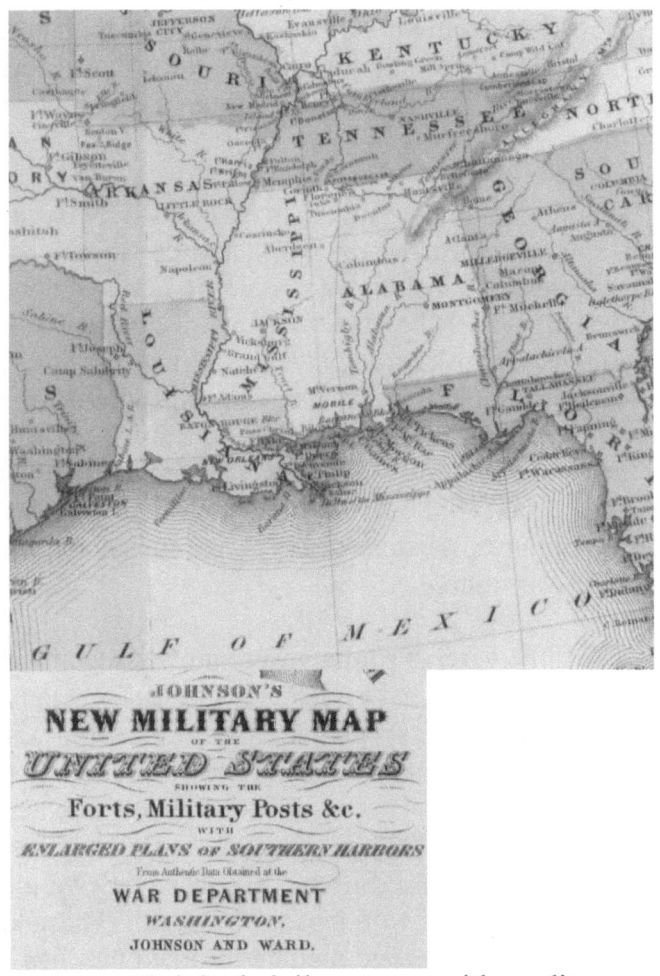

Original civil war map with credit

The men never talked about the torture they endured for nearly six months, but they did talk about the different locations they traveled, particularly the ocean at the Gulf of Mexico. They also talked about

New Orleans but not of Elsie's house in the French Quarter. The young kids loved to hear these stories, as did several young ladies that the men knew before they left for war.

As previously mentioned, in early 1865, Missouri was a split state because the North and the South were represented there. Town people would have neighbors that fought for the other side than what their children fought. It was hard to put this stinking war away, even here at home. Everything seemed to be affected badly, but no more than the injured soldiers that could no longer help on the farms. Over the next few years, many good soldiers would die painful deaths due to their injuries. History doesn't talk much about the post-war injured.

The three veteran soldiers were getting together every few evenings to have a hoot of a time. They loved that Kentucky bourbon and many liquor stills also popped up all over Missouri. They just couldn't kick their bad habits. The young ladies they knew before the war had not changed that much, and they were disgusted by these drinking habits, so they wouldn't go to the "Hoot" with these wilder ones. These ladies were hoping for good men that wanted families, and it seemed that the war destroyed these three men.

Anyway, while the hooting and drinking went on each week, the three would also hunt for food. While hunting with friends, Jonny tells others to shoot to kill fast. Don't torture these animals like we were during that "Consarn" war. The three men were hunting on the way backcountry, so-as no one would know what they had done. Jonny reiterated to the others that they were here to get meat so that we could eat and have fun, and we were not here to torture the animals. Let's just have a clean hit, a clean kill, and then we can eat, but Bobby (still the worst of the three) saw the first deer and took a wild shot at the back end of the deer just to slow it down. It did not go down right away. It ran as much as its adrenaline would let it, thrashing on the ground in severe pain. Jonny loudly said, "What the "Consarn" are you doing, you Hog Shit. I told you not to do that; you shoot to kill, not to wound." The good man Jonny then walked up to the deer in pain and quickly put the deer out of his misery. He then walked back to Bobby and, without saying anything, slammed his fists into Bobby's nose. They were all pretty drunk then, so Bobby didn't feel anything, but Bobby fell to the ground quickly with his nose bleeding and clearly bent. Jonny then said, "I'm leaving now," and started walking away. At this time, Will (the third young man) said. "NO, don't do it! DON'T SHOOT", and a loud bang came from Bobby's gun. Jonny fell to the ground with his left shoulder decimated by the larger caliber bullet. Jonny then reached for his new handgun, turned, and got one shot off before he died. The shot was right-on and dead-center in the head of Bobby.

Jonny's Soul went to the Higgs Field. Unfortunately, the Soul of Jonny didn't learn much from this life, but it did learn of compassion for animals based on the horrors he witnessed firsthand in the Civil War.

Substance abuse and the war destroyed much of the person called "Jonny."

Note: The only person that survived this gunfight was Will. He was already good and drunk and confused as hell. He grabbed the bottle of bourbon and drank solidly until he passed out.

Later that night, a mountain lion found his past-out body. Will moved a little prompting the big cat to grab Will by the throat and suffocate him to death. Will did struggle a little, but he was just too drunk. Will made it to the Higgs Field and the Whole-One, but Bobby didn't.

Photo (by author) taken at the Denver Museum of Nature and Science

Sub-Chapter 6D: 1880 Year Man - learns of humility and to not act on revenge.

In 1870, it was a wild time in what will be South Dakota, particularly the Black Hills. The Federal Government had difficulties handling settlers in the West as more people sought fortunes and homesteading. The Government mainly saw the Indian Tribes as an obstacle, so they sent armies of hardened soldiers to the West to so-called "Civilize" the area. Most of these soldiers were in the Civil War and used to war. This decision was just business for Congress.

The Sioux Nation had been in this area for untold years, and over these years, the seven larger tribes of the Sioux Nation had roughly established hunting boundaries. The seven Sioux tribes were the Wdewakanton, Sisseton, Teton (or Lakota), Wahpekute, Wahpeton, Yankton, and Yanktonai.

A child was born in the Lakota Sioux Tribe just after the Civil War, in late 1865. His name was Hotah. His father was Jai, meaning "Victorious," and his mother was Amrita, which means "Immortality." They had their son in the southern Black Hills, near many hot springs (today, this is the area around Hot Springs, South Dakota). He was the only son of his folks, although they wanted a big family. The Tribe always encouraged childbearing. The bigger the Tribe, the safer they were from nearby tribes.

Although white settlers were already in the Black Hills, this specific area didn't receive too much conflict. The gold rush within the hills wouldn't occur until the mid-1870s, so this Tribe mainly saw homesteaders, wagon trains, and the occasional fur trappers. The Chiefs of the Tribe noticed an uptick of white settlers, which was disturbing, but most conflicts occurred up north and to the West. The Band that Hotah was a part of didn't know the reasons for these conflicts.

The White Man was active in acquiring land at this time, but the Indian People didn't know anything about land ownership, and they didn't even know what this meant. They didn't mind some of those traveling through to get food and water as needed. They didn't own the land and understood that no human could ever own it. They had their hunting areas to defend, but passers-by were not an issue. They knew they didn't own the land but used it for food and water.

The Federal Government didn't have a problem with the Indian people occupying the Black Hills until gold was found. It was this single event that caused the Federal Government to backtrack on previous agreements to allow white settlers to dig for this valuable mineral. It helped the Government become more financially stable, and as stated before, the Government didn't think of the Indian People as Americans, even though they were the first, true Americans.

Hotah grew up in the southern hills. The group he was born in was a smaller Band of about 30 people, and they were much more nomadic than most other Lakota people. They traveled from what is now the Wyoming side of the Black Hills to the middle eastern edge, where Rapid City is now. Hotah loved the hills in all seasons. Of course, travel in winter was more difficult, but there were always warmer winter days too. At age 10, he learned his way around very well. It was as if he had a compass in his head.

The Lakota Tribe was not ruthless but would defend itself powerfully if needed. Much land separated the bands of the Lakota Tribe, but they remained united and helped each Band out when necessary. Fortunately, these were rugged people, and help was rarely needed. The total Lakota Tribe population during the time of Hotah was about 16,000.

When Hotah was 11, news of the Battle of Little Big Horn was unnerving. Although the Lakota warriors won the battle, it told of a war between the white people and the Indian people, and then when Hotah was 12, the news of the killing of Crazy Horse was devastating. Shortly after this, Hotah met Sitting Bull in person and eventually became a scout for him while Sitting Bull was in the southern Hills.

The death of these great warriors molded Hotah's opinion to some degree. All of the Lakota Tribe and all of the Sioux Nation understood life on the plains and the Black Hills. Then, when others came to take it away, the Nation needed to defend these hunting grounds. It was their lives and livelihood that they were defending.

At age 15, Hotah knew all he could from his nomadic people. He was strong, smart, understanding, and a quick learner at such an early age. At this age, he would leave by himself for days just to feel the mystery of the Black Hills. Gaining food and water was easy for him, given the skills from his Band. Now, he needed to understand his purpose for the Tribe. Days would go by as he walked the deer trails in the hills and saw wonderful sights, such as a cave with a 4-foot-wide ice pillar from ground to ceiling. This sight might not be unusual in winter, but he witnessed it in July. He called this Ice Cave, just as it's called today. This location became his camp for about a week, and he loved every minute of it. He felt this to be the center of his universe. At night he would look up into the dark sky, see the lights above, and wonder what they were. Occasionally he saw one of them decide to cross the sky for him. This area was on religious grounds and must be protected.

Photo (by author) of southern Black Hills taken in
December 2021

As he traveled back to the Band, he camped at many
sites. Rain would fall over parts of the hills, and he
could see the large clouds build up over the higher
elevations. Then, hours later, he could hear thunder
underground as the rainwater flowed in large amounts
through the complex network of caverns that were cut
out over the millennia via the erosion of limestone.

- SPECIAL REFERENCE: The Island in the
  Plains, A Black Hills Natural History, by
  Edward Raventon, 1994, Johnson Printing
  Company

Hotah was at home in the hills and the surrounding
plains. He could not envision anything else.

Back at his Band, he told of his explorations, and
most of the Band listened, but one young woman
seemed especially interested, and it wasn't just the

stories she was interested in. Hotah noticed and reciprocated. He had noticed her many times before. Her name was Wichapi. It was kind of unusual for Hotah, but he liked her independence, and they started seeing each other. It started slowly initially, but they couldn't wait to get together after a short time. Within a month, they would be man and wife, but they were anything but normal. They would spend as much time in the remote hills as possible, and Hotah eventually showed Wichapi the Ice Cave. It would become their special spot in the southern hills.

In August of the first year that Hotah and Wichapi were together, they visited the Ice Cave again, but this time they climbed to the top of the cave entrance and watched the sunset. It was absolutely beautiful. They slept outside under the stars that night and watched hundreds of lights cross the sky above them (called the Perseids Meteor Shower today). In the morning, they both watched the sun come up over the Black Hills to what would be another perfect day in the hills, the best physical environment that could ever exist on planet earth.

Hotah and Wichapi were on top of the world. They shared such special places and enjoyed being with one another. It was the best of times for them both. How did life get so good? Their health and love seemed to flourish daily, and they could see nothing that could damage their relationship. Imagine being in the paradise of the Black Hills in the summertime, being young and healthy, and having the ability to get food and water with little effort.

It really was paradise. Love and the freedom to go where ever they wanted. They also loved the night sky, which seemed to shine with bright lights even without the moon, and one night they saw so many lights crossing the sky that they thought the sky was dancing for them. It was the Garden of Eden for them that August and they could not see anything changing. Even back with their Lakota Band, and in winter, things seemed so easy and simple. This is the way life should be for everyone, Hotah thought. Why did things seem so different before? But he knew the answer; his life with Wichapi had changed everything for him.

Food was no problem for these two while they were exploring. They weren't hungry often, but Hotah decided to trap a bird for dinner while at the Ice Cave. He had experience catching ducks on ponds, and he knew of a pond nearby. Sure enough, two ducks were on this small pond. Hotah used his bow to shoot a small arrow, which was on target. The other duck flew off, and Hotah and Wichapi started to clean off the feathers. It was then that Hotah noticed the other duck circling above. Wichapi asked Hotah, "Do ducks mate for life, like us?" Hotah had never once thought of this. Was she right? He did not know, but he did know to give thanks for the meal and thank the great spirits for the nourishment. It was sad for them both, but food is needed for survival and life.

Wichapi had a way of making Hotah think of things that he had never thought of before. She was wonderful for Hotah. He then started to think of all the animals he killed over the years, and he vowed to give respect for future kills that would keep him alive and well. It was the way of many Lakota to give thanks like this, and now he knows why. He knew that someday his body would also nourish wild animals. It was the circle of life.

Within a short time, Hotah and Wichapi talked about starting a family. They were so happy it was unimaginable, but then Hotah started returning off his high. He knew of the increasing numbers of white settlers and the impending danger, and he remembered the long nights listening to Sitting Bull and his unimaginable predictions of impending disaster. It was no time to raise a family. It was the time to plan for the worst.

The honeymoon was over for Hotah and Wichapi, and they came crashing back to earth. Fortunately, they were realists and knew what real life was about in the 1880s.

Over time, Hotah and Wichapi would investigate the caverns that Hotah knew existed from the thundering rivers he heard underground after large rainfalls. It was difficult at first because it was so dark not far from the cave entrances, but somehow Hotah acquired a special gift of starting fires, and they went further back into the caves. They would do this in winter when hunting season slowed for the Band, and the caves were always the same temperature all year long, so winter was the same as summer for their cave exploration. It was incredible! Now they had protection from the weather and any enemies above. They would just need to be aware of the flowing water from rain storms, and they did find many places underground that didn't have the flowing stormwater. It would prove invaluable for his Band during what is called the "Indian Wars."

Oddly enough, one of these caves is now located in modern-day Custer State Park and is called Wind Cave National Park, but Custer didn't know of the caves that would eventually protect Hotah & Wichapi and their Band of Lakota people. How ironic and serendipitous.

The war of the late 1800s was devastating to the Indian people of the Black Hills and surrounding grasslands. Many of the experienced Civil War soldiers were ruthless in their killing. Many came to love killing as a sport and didn't see the Indian people as real people. Unfortunately, the Federal Government either didn't know this or didn't care at the time. Back in Washington, DC, they just wanted the Indian problem to go away. Custer didn't do it, so more was needed. To the disadvantage of the Lakota people, technology was changing rapidly during this time, and it produced the chambered gun. The Indian people could fight against the musket, but chambered bullets could kill far more in such a short period. The Indian people did not have a chance against this new technology.

Although the Indian Lakota people were rugged, strong, and skilled, they were not ruthless people.

They would give benefit-of-doubt before making rash decisions to fight. This respect is what often led to their defeat when more ruthless people would attack without any warning or reason; other than that, they were just Indian people, but the Lakota learned from these early attacks and became more defensive, not letting their guard down.

More United States soldiers were sent out west to "Civilize" the Black Hills, as they put it to newspapers in the Eastern States, and we all know what evolved into Indian Reservations, but you don't know of the hide-out Band of Lakota people, thanks to Hotah and Wichapi.

Southern Black Hills, picture taken in December 2021 by author

It was late in the year 1880 when Hotah could see the early signs of an attack from the white man. He noticed unusual movements of some animals while hunting, and occasionally he would see a white man leaving an area, perhaps a scout for the white man's Army. Hotah had earlier learned these signs from animals during late-hour talks around the open fire with Sitting Bull. Hotah was astute to animal movements as a result. He had dreams of watching and learning about animal movements. It was told that he would become one with the animal he pursued.

Something was clearly going on, and they needed more information about any potential invasion. Hotah and Wichapi could not be everywhere all of the time, so they employed young Indian scouts that would live in various parts of the southern hills and report back if something unusual happened and it was this effort that led to the understanding of a very large army of blue soldiers coming in from the east.

The news spread fast through his Band, and food was preserved and brought to the cave entrance for eventual storage. Water wasn't a problem because water constantly dripped from the ceiling of the caves everywhere. Food was stored by the tons, and it was smoked and salted meats, herbs, and grass for animals. It was a sight to behold, and you wouldn't believe it. It was like the Book of Noah in the Bible, storing away food in a Wooden Ark. They had food for months at least.

It seemed the cave would go on forever and split many times. Other holes and surface entrances were found, and the Band covered these so that no one could stumble upon them, but the holes provided plenty of fresh air and escape routes if needed.

As the Federal soldiers approached and were about two days away, the Band of Lakota started their occupation of the caves. Small fires were placed at key locations to allow some light, but they kept them small on purpose to not have large amounts of smoke from escaping the caves. Most family campsites within the caves were near openings so that some light came in without fires, and when the soldiers were close, all fires were put out.

Sounds made in the caves were not easily heard outside of the caves because of the rocks and earth. This made for a stealthier hideout.

Two spots were used as overview lookouts. Both were vertical holes from the caves, about 2 feet in diameter each. Hotah and some others took two hollowed-out stumps and placed them over the holes. They then positioned some spy holes at various areas of the stump to see out over the land. It would become crucial for letting the Band know when they needed to be in the caves. Although they slept in the caves each night, they would go outside when the white soldiers were not nearby. After all, they really didn't know if the soldiers were there to capture or kill them or if the soldiers were just passing through.

The Lakota Indian Band finished preparation as the soldiers were just one day out. This break gave them plenty of time to cover up any signs of them being in or around the caves. They left their old camp in shambles just to give the impression that they moved out in haste, and even placed many signs of them leaving for areas west, in what is now Wyoming.

The day the soldiers were to arrive had come. The Lakota Band, now about 50 strong, was well prepared. Two lookouts were placed at the stump lookouts, and then they waited and hoped that these soldiers were just passing by. One lookout had a great view of where the pines met the plains and where the town of Buffalo Gap, South Dakota, is today. This higher ground overlook was always the best and favorite spot for the Lakota Band to see if the Buffalo was approaching in past years and decades.

The lookout scout saw the soldiers coming from the east, and it was easy to see with all of the dust. It was a good-sized army of about 100 men. Why would so many soldiers be traveling this way?

It was about an hour from when the soldiers would be at their closest to the main cave entrance when the lookout scout sent an alarming message to Hotah. The scout saw another small Band of Lakota traveling directly toward where the soldiers were heading.

"No!!!", Hotah said in his native language; this is horrible. He told everyone to stay in the caves and that he would try to warn the other Lakota Band. Hotah was a fast runner, but this would take everything he had to get to the Band before being seen by the soldiers. He ran like lightning down the hills and over the small hogback just in time to see that the soldiers had already spotted the Lakota Band.

This small Lakota Band was stunned to see so many soldiers traveling toward them with such speed. They panicked and started to run towards the hogback that Hotah had just arrived at. Hotah yelled to them to come up the hill, and they came as fast as they could, but the woman and children were much slower at arriving, and the soldiers caught up to them easily. Hotah thought they would be taken captive, but to his horror, they were cut down as they ran. It was shocking to see this, but now Hotah knew their true intentions to eliminate the Indian people.

Those that made it up to his position were exhausted, but they had to continue now or be killed. Rather than go straight to the main entrance, Hotah was forced to take an alternate route to have the soldier chase them away from the cave entrances. It was a difficult choice because he knew many of these people would be unable to keep up enough to stay ahead of the soldiers, but what else could he do? As they continued up the hill, they heard screams of pain and death. It was a nightmare. The strongest and fastest from this Band were still with Hotah, and they zig-zagged through the pines and were eventually able to temporarily escape the Army. Only 5 of this Band made it; four were men, and one was a woman. They were all distraught and in shock, not to mention worn out and dehydrated. Then, from behind a bush, they heard a noise. It was Wichapi with a couple of other men from their Band. Wichapi told Hotah to stay down and that she and the other two men would lay a trail in the opposite direction of the caves so that Hotah and the other five survivors could get to freedom via the cave entrance.

Hotah didn't like his wife taking this risk, but he was completely exhausted. Wichapi and the other two warriors then took off, silent at first, and then when they were far enough from Hotah and the survivors, they got louder to attract attention. IT WORKED! The army soldiers fell for it and followed Wichapi and the warriors.

After the soldiers were far enough away, Hotah took the five survivors to the cave for rest and treatment.

It wasn't any problem for Wichapi and the other two warriors to evade the soldiers because they knew the area well. Also, the soldiers did not have as much to lose, so they were slower.

A few hours later, Wichapi and the two brave warriors entered the cave, safe and sound, and the Federal Army had no idea where they went, but they did know they were out there somewhere, and that would be a problem, but just not now.

It was almost a panicked situation within the cave as Hotah's Band and the five other Band members were united. It was good that the soldiers weren't around the cave openings because everyone was so excited. Not just for the survival of the 5 Band members but outrage for these innocents that were cut down for no reason.

Later as they became more organized, one of the lookout scouts told what he had seen during this chaotic time. As Hotah ran out towards the small

Band of Lakota, the scout said that it was not all of the soldiers that chased after them. He said that most of the regiment of soldiers simply stayed in formation after seeing one group chase the Indian Band. In fact, most of the soldiers stayed in place. At one point, the lookout scout saw a leader of the soldiers go back to one of the formations that held back, take out what appeared to be a pistol, and drop the lead soldier to the ground. The other soldiers behind the one that was killed scattered. This information told Hotah that the white soldiers were not united in their attempt to kill them, and he thought he might use this to his advantage.

Meanwhile, back at the Federal Army, the units were re-gathering, with the exception of a dozen or so soldiers that took off eastwards, leaving a trail of dust.

It was getting dark, so the Army decided to make camp near where Buffalo Gap is today, but on the other side of the hogback, closer to the pines and a pond of water. The camp seemed organized, but loud noises were heard from time to time, and at least two-gun shots were heard.

Both sides were exhausted, so nothing more happened that night, but it was assured that the Army would be back looking for the survivors in the morning.

Hotah knew how to gain the advantage and also how to draw the Army away from the cave entrances. Early the next morning, he gathered 3 of his best bow

& arrow shooters. They positioned themselves on the edge of the hogback, opposite the pines, next to where the hog-back borders the prairie. They waited and watched the Army come to life and start breakfast and the take-down of the camp. They were in no hurry, so Hotah and others watched and had their own food and water. Two bodies were taken away from the camp and buried, so they assumed what the two-gun shots were about that previous evening, which was encouraging to Hotah. He knew that not all white men would accept cold-blooded murder.

As they watched the Army break down camp, he could definitely see who the commander was, and he watched to see what horse he had. Fortunately, the horse was very noticeable; it was a beautiful white animal.

Near where the Army camped, there is a part of the hogback that is a cliff on the side facing the Black Hills with an easy slope on the prairie side. The camp was in between the hogback and the pines of the Black Hills, so this was the absolute perfect place to get a few arrows off and still be far enough away. In addition, they could simply head out into the prairie before the Army could travel around the hogback to catch them.

NOTE: You can see the aerial view of this spot-on Google Earth by looking for Buffalo Gap, South Dakota. The small pond near the highway is near where the Army camped, and the town is on the other side of the small hogback. Hotah and the archers positioned themselves at the peak of this small hogback.

Photo (by author) taken December 2021. The town of Buffalo Gap is just over the ridge (hogback)

When the Army started its early formation, Hotah decided this was the best time to remove the main commander. He asked each archer to have three arrows to show in quick order and to only shoot at the commander.

It happened this way…. As the Army started in formation, Hotah stood on the edge of the hogback and yelled in his language, "Half-Man Murderers". The Army didn't know what he said, but that got their attention. The Army commander made the mistake of charging up toward the cliff side of the hogback, and this is exactly what Hotah wanted. When they realized they couldn't ride up that side of the hogback, Hotah told his archers to shoot at will. The first couple of arrows fell short, which helped the archers with distance and wind. The third archer made the hit on the commander, but it wasn't a fatal blow, only to the shoulder. The first two archers re-loaded, and those two made their mark. The commander didn't know what hit him, and he fell off his horse. The horse was unharmed, and the other soldiers didn't know what to do. One officer said, "Go through the gap" (meaning the Buffalo Gap), and they did, but when they got to the other side, Hotah and the three archers were well on their way out of sight.

Hotah and the three archers traveled south into the grasslands to what is now called Spring Creek. They then followed the creak westward and back to the pines. They then went up to the cave entrance. It was a long trip and took two days, but well worth it so that the Army wouldn't find their cave hideouts.

While Hotah and the three archers were en route, the Army was observed to be in flux. The next high-level officer and his subordinate officers tried to gain control, but the radical approach of cutting down innocent Indian people was more than most of the hardened Civil War soldiers could take. Most of the soldiers did not participate in the attack on innocent Indian people, but about ten did. These ten soldiers were the worst of the worst and fought together in the Civil War with the same Captain. Rumor was that they even tortured confederate soldiers that were captured. After about two hours, control was achieved, but they now had two different groups of soldiers that disagreed with one another, and this split the Army. To maintain some kind of discipline, they divided the soldiers into two groups. The larger group continued west, through the hills to the grasslands on the other side. They then traveled up the west side of the Black Hills in search of other Indian camps. If found, they were instructed to lead them to areas of land that would eventually become reservations. The smaller group of hardened soldiers was to search for Hotah and the three archers. After all, ten soldiers should be more than enough to catch four Indians.

The ten soldiers, including two officers, followed the tracks as far as possible. At Spring Creek, they lost the trail. They could see that the four Indians could travel downstream towards the prairie or upstream towards the pines. They, of course, traveled towards the pines and looked for any evidence of tracks coming out of the creek. It took two days, but they did finally find some evidence of human tracks leaving the creek for the north, back deeper into the Black Hills. Unfortunately for the soldiers, the tracks were extremely hard to follow due to rock outcrops and the cover of pine needles. The ten soldiers spread out and moved north slowly and did stay somewhat on the same path that Hotah and the others stayed on.

The noise made by the soldiers was surprising to the Lakota scouts because they were easy to see and hear coming from a long distance. They were sloppy and arrogant to think that they had the upper hand in this situation. The Indians allowed these soldiers to come deep into the area where several cave openings were, and the soldiers didn't suspect a thing.

At the hoot of an owl, arrows started flying from all directions onto the Union soldiers. Many Indian warriors were positioned in trees, and others charged out of the cave openings. The soldiers were caught completely off-guard, just like Custer and the 7th Calvary Regiment did earlier, in 1876. Only one of the soldiers survived the rage that the Lakota felt towards those that murdered the innocent. Hotah was the first to notice that this older officer was not hit with any arrow and was not injured at all. As Hotah walked up to the old officer, the officer pleaded for his life, and he was visibly shaking. Hotah knew a little of the English language from trading with the good white settlers, so Hotah asked the officer what his name was. The officer stuttered out, "My name is Captain Clark." It was obvious that this officer was scared out of his mind. It was the first time Captain Clark was ever on the receiving side of captivity.

Historic photo of the Custer expedition from about 1874.

Hotah slowly walked around Captain Clark as others in the tribe spit on him and kicked him occasionally. Then Hotah held up his arms and told Clark to walk out of the Black Hills and tell his army that the Lakota are merciful to those who show mercy.

Captain Clark's gun, belt, hat, and knife were taken from him, and he was allowed to leave the area.

Captain Clark never made it out of the hills. He always had other lower-ranking soldiers do the hard work of gaining food and water and setting up camp with fire. Although he had done these things in the past, he was a ruthless officer and never kept up with these skills. Also, he was often drunk when liquor was available. Captain Clark died of exposure and was food for the wild animals. Captain Clark never made it to the Higgs Field.

That was it for this battle, and this small Band of Lakota celebrated the victory and freedom, but they all knew that more soldiers would come, so they were vigilant.

As the months passed, no soldiers came. However, white settlers did, and so did many prospectors for gold in the northern hills near where Lead, South Dakota, is now. The Gold Rush was on, and although Hotah and his Band of Lakota were in the southern hills, they still saw some effect. There were so many white settlers and prospectors that this small Band of Lakota was clearly outnumbered. This disparity had a huge negative outcome on the hunting grounds, but Hotah insisted they share the land rather than fight. After all, who would they be fighting, family settlers? As mentioned earlier, this Band of Lakota were reasonable and would not attack the innocent, but they could maintain most of the hunting grounds for food and went further out from the hills as needed for buffalo. That worked for about a decade.

When Hotah was in his thirties, he and Wichapi had two boys. The oldest was 11, and the youngest was 10 years old. They both were already good hunters and travelers. Although Hotah would have liked his sons to be older before he took them on difficult hunting trips, he felt the need to make them men as soon as possible. Hotah could see that the life he and the Lakota had lived in the past was coming to an end. Hotah wanted his family to live free, and for this reason, he had many conversations with nearby white settlers that had become friendly with his Band.

Friendships continued to build between this Band of Lakota and the surrounding white neighbors, and they even traded together. Unfortunately, not all white prospectors felt this way. The prospectors wanted to see if gold could be found in the area where the Lakota camped, and this was also the area of their caves, but the white settlers didn't know about the caves.

One day, Hotah was out hunting with his two sons when they heard a loud gunshot. The boys looked behind them and saw two prospectors, one with a gun that was just shot. Then they saw Hotah on the ground, bleeding. As he lay on the ground, his sons were frantic to keep him alive. Hotah then went into a trance and heard a voice in his head say,…. "You are now **Brahman**. You will not be reborn again. Your new name is "**Miha**," given to you from the many times we have been together."

Hotah opened his eyes for the last time within 3D+T and said, "**I am Miha**."

The Soul, during the life of Hotah, learned of humility and compassion. The Soul entered the Higgs field immediately. It would not emerge again. Miha was now fully a part of the Whole-One, and would eventually see his sons, Wichapi, and most of the Lakota Nation enters the Higgs Field and the Whole-One. He also saw many of his white settler friends come through the Higgs Field.

Chapter 7: MIXED FEELING

SPECIAL NOTE: Although Miha was a man in all of his 3D+T lives, the real experience in life is not subject to sex in the eyes of the Whole-One. Experiences are for the Whole-One, and sex is only a physical thing for the reproduction of the species. It really doesn't matter to the Higgs Field or the Whole-One. Sex is only for the 3D+T world.

Bret didn't know what to think or feel; how could he? And even Miha said that his words were just the best interpretation possible. The human experiences were totally different than what Bret thought previously, and Bret wondered how others would interpret things if they had learned what he had.

Miha said, "Well, now you know a little of the last lives my Soul had. I hope this helps you understand."

This new information did help greatly, but Bret had more questions.

Bret asked, "Miha, one main question has always been on my mind, why are some babies stillborn or die from some disease shortly after birth? It doesn't make sense that a Soul would come to the 3D+T and die without any experiences."

Miha told Bret that he had seen many children and newly born animals enter the Higgs Barrier but could only partially answer Bret's question. "I can't relay to you why a Soul returns so quickly back to the Whole-One. I've seen this same Soul be reborn to parents in their very next child's birth, but other Souls do come as different people within different families at different times. The Whole-One chooses the Soul's destiny on the other side of the Higgs Barrier. The Soul's return is subject to causality and determinism within your 4-space. Having lived many lives, I do remember it seems cruel, and I'm sorry that I can't give you more information, but any detailed explanation would not make sense to you in your world. Bret, things are much different here in this Higgs Barrier, and more so on the side of the Whole-One, but I will tell you that Love and Kindness are on the side of the Whole-One, and you would not want to leave there if you didn't need to experience more lives. Life gives experience, and that is what is needed to become **Brahman.**"

Miha continued, "Bret, would it surprise you if I told you that your Soul has been with the Whole-One several times already? I can't tell you any more other than the Whole-One is happy with your Soul. I have met your Soul and those that temporarily housed your Soul. We have been together many times before, and I've always enjoyed being with you."

"It is unfortunate that more souls don't cross over to Brahman, but I know those from all over the universe, and so many animals that you call pets do cross over. It appears to me that goodness and honesty help to become Brahman, but there is more. Understanding and compassion is also key factor, and not just for your kind. All animals experience play and comfort. All animals love in their own way."

"In the 3D+T world, most needed to take a life for nourishment, but those that did this with respect were the ones that the Whole-One noticed. Living simply for pleasure is not the answer. Life must be respected, and honor must be given to those that are taken for food. Don't worry, those taken for food will be back in the 3D+T soon enough, and you'd be surprised to see the enormous times that the situation is reversed. When those realize this in the Higgs Field, it changes them, and they become more Brahman. Then, life continues. Those that learn, return to more lives for more experience. You can see this is much more complicated than you might imagine, but it's really a beautiful process, and Bret, you'll love the love in the Whole-One. It is like nothing you'll ever experience in the 3D+T."

"Bret, I hope you can understand this difficult discussion. You have been given the gift of this conversation."

Later, Bret perfected his communication experiment as best he could, and actively sought out others that experienced grief. Others that were reasonable thinking people that might be able to shed more light on this wonderful gift of an experiment. Bret and his wife Barb knew of one individual that they trusted with this secret. He was a family member. His name was Nick.

Nick was in a wheelchair for most of his life. He had been in a terrible accident when he was young; that was not his fault. In his early life, Nick had difficulty in his condition but was strong-willed and determined to live a good life. He was brought up in a low-income part of town and even had to defend himself from rougher kids that didn't care that he was in a wheelchair. He even carried a weapon with him for protection in his neighborhood. This hardship made him tougher, but he never lost his humanity. He was a caring person, and people could always depend on him. His determination prospered, and he became self-sufficient. Others in his condition would not have. He was smart, to be sure, but it was really his determination that helped him survive.

He was nothing short of amazing, and if anyone deserved to meet Miha, it was Nick. Also, Nick became proficient at computers with both software and hardware. He didn't have formal training, but he knew more than most that received bachelor's degrees in Computer Science. His computer knowledge also made him the perfect One to help with the system, including the cooling system. Nick read a lot when he wasn't on the computer and knew how to research better than anyone. If anyone could improve on Bret's setup, Nick could.

However, Nick lived in another state at the time, but Bret and Barb knew that Nick would move back once he saw this amazing setup, and he loved Colorado too. So, they flew Nick back to Colorado to show him the setup and make introductions.

Bret and Barb introduced him to Miha. Nick was astounded, to say the least. He was only the third person to ever see beyond the 3D+T. The three of them needed a private space to communicate with Miha independently and not in Bret and Barb's home, so they decided to rent a space to communicate with Miha privately. They knew that what was said would be deeply personal. Although they knew Nick, they didn't know his inner thoughts. Privacy was important to everyone.

Bret and Barb trusted Nick to become the gatekeeper of this rented space. It was secure, and all three of them had keys, so anyone of them could communicate in private with Miha. They all agreed to take precautions to not let this new setup be known to others. They had two passwords, and the system needed to be turned on in a specific sequence, or it would not work. Miha agreed, even though if someone else did turn this system on, it wouldn't work. Miha would make sure of that. Miha didn't say this, though. The more precautions, the better.

Nick was always one of his favorite family members to both, Bret and Barb, so this situation made them closer, and Nick was very appreciative of Bret and Barb for this incredible experience. He was able to communicate with the loved ones that he had lost, and he regained his thrill of life.

With Nick taking care of the equipment now and also keeping this secret, Bret and Barb started to travel during their retirement years. They traveled to spots that they knew were past lives of Miha. They traveled to Canada (just above Michigan), to northern Michigan, then to Springfield, Missouri, Tennessee, Atlanta, the Gulf Coast, and New Orleans. Lastly, they, of course, visited the Black Hills of South Dakota, including Buffalo Gap and eastern Wyoming too. It was all fascinating, knowing what happened at these locations many years ago. They knew Miha was with them at each of these places even though they didn't have the equipment to communicate. It was a fantastic and fun trip. They stayed the last few days in Rapid City, South Dakota, in order to visit Sturgis, and yes, they needed to see Mount Rushmore too. To their surprise, they learned of the Crazy Horse monument, and this was much more interesting to them since Hotah mentioned him. This was an amazing sight and made the trip well worth it, but they also had to visit Wind Cave, knowing how the Lakota Band had used the cave system to survive the Union Army attack.

Photo of eastern Wyoming - December 2021

The crowds of tourists didn't bother them; they just

thought it funny how people marveled at these sites in the Black Hills.

They had one more site to visit, which was much more important. It was harder to get to, and they needed a quadrangle map to find it. It was Ice-Cave. When they drove up to this location, they were surprised at the large entrance. They expected a smaller opening and even bought spelunking equipment to go inside. They didn't even need a flashlight to see where the ice was in the past. It had a frozen wet spot on the ground from dripping water. There was a smaller opening in the back of this large opened-mouthed cave for more exploration, but they just stayed in the larger part. This larger opening was opposite where the sun shined, so ice could easily have formed in the past, even in summer. They were disappointed not to find the pillar of ice, but on the Internet, they found pictures of the ice from the 1970s or early 1980s, but nothing now.

Bret and Barb camped there for three nights and looked up at the stars as Hotah & Wichapi did more than 100 years ago. It was gorgeous, and it was paradise on earth, without any doubt. Barb even seemed to remember events like this before in her life but couldn't remember when. Probably something she did with her folks when she was growing up. They then hiked the area and even found the pond where Hotah killed the duck. The pond didn't have much water in it, and it wasn't frozen over, but at least it was there. Just for fun, Bret and Barb skinny-dipped in the pond even though it was a colder time of year, and they had a fire to warm up after getting out. It was exhilarating. They knew Miha would be aware of this, but they also knew that Miha remembered the good times of the 3D+T. At the bottom of this shallow pond, Bret found a small arrowhead. It must have been from Hotah. It was an unexpected treasure from the past.

They also slept in the cave one night. It was like they were early cave-people or something prehistoric, and the sleep and dreams were better than ever. They dreamed of star-filled nights and meteor showers. It was funny that they both had the same dreams.

The last night at the Ice Cave, Bret produced a bottle of Kentucky Bourbon. It was Westford Reserve. That night they drank and danced around a fire until midnight. Then they slept close to one another all night long under a star-filled night and watched the meteors dash across the sky. How strange it was for them to see the same things as others from the past and feel the same wonder of things. Yes, they know the lights that fly by are meteors, and the ones that are stationary are either stars or planets. The main thing is that these are beautiful and are for our pleasure, no matter what century we live in. Both Bret and Barb realized that night that they were only on this earth for experience and that they would not be here for long. They enjoyed the night sky until sun-up, as it was an unusually warm winter day. Then they slept in the warmth of the sun as it rose up to about 10:00 AM.

They made a late breakfast on an open fire, just as Hotah & Wichapi would have done with the duck. They thanked Miha and the Whole-One for this wonderful vacation and started to pack up, but they didn't want to leave. Something was holding them back, but they ignored it. They needed to get back home to their modern lives. They forced themselves to pack and took many pictures for memories and to show Nick what a great place this was. Perhaps they would visit again, next time, with Nick. They cleaned up the site as if no one was there, and they got in their car.

Now it was time for them to head home. Even though it was early winter, it was warmer than usual, and the radio weather channel only talked of scattered snow showers. No problem for Bret; he grew up in this area and had driven through many blizzards. On the way home to Colorado, they were traveling just past Mule Creek Junction in Wyoming, and a snow squall appeared out of nowhere. Bret had driven in much worse conditions and just slowed down and kept the wheels on any dry roadway that he could.

It was nearly a white-out situation when their car was hit head-on by a semi-truck driver that was in the wrong lane.

Bret looked at Barb, and she looked at him. They were both still together, but they were no longer in the car. They held each other's hands as they seemed to float up to where they both saw a familiar face. It was Miha, and he was with many others. There was the man that Tasky had walked within the Middle East just before he was killed, and so many others, including both their parents, and old friends that had passed before them, and many other good people that both Bret and Barb had known over the years while living in the 3D+T. It was also a surprise to see others that they knew during other lives that they lived. They could now remember all of the lives that their Sole occupied. There were so many, and so many memories of the past lives lived.

It was not just Bret that became Brahman; it was Barb too. You see, Barb had many lives, including Ish, from the time of 10,000 years ago, and she was Avigal during the time of Jesus Christ. She was also Wichapi during the 1880s in the Black Hills of South Dakota. You see, she was with Miha all of these lives, but she needed one more. The Whole-One and Miha put Bret and Barb together because of their goodness and kindness, as well as to make their physical lives easier in their last lives within the physical world. It was beautiful.

As they traveled through the Higgs Barrier, they hesitated. This was happening so fast for them, and they were still experiencing TIME. They knew Nick would be watching from the computer set-up, and they wanted him to know all was okay. They waved at him as they entered the Whole-One for the last time. They also said they would be waiting for him, even though TIME would not exist for them within the Whole-One, but they knew that would be comforting for Nick.

Nick was both sad and happy at the same time. What a mixture of emotions. He was extremely grievous and also laughed out loud at the very same time. He lost two of his many best friends, but he also knew that hope was there for him in the 3D+T world, and he looked forward to the time he could join them. He hoped that he was close to Brahman too, but before he left this 3D+T existence, he knew what his mission in life was. Bret and Barb had entrusted him with a miracle machine and a great interpreter named Miha.

Nick wanted to help other people that were in deep grief. He knew many from the hospital staff that helped him, but he had to be selective. This was a powerful tool, and he needed to keep it safe. He knew of one nurse that was exceptional in the care for and of her patients. She was well-regarded and had worked tirelessly for years with COVID patients. She was certainly one of a select few that Nick considered introducing to Miha, but Nick needed to check with Miha first.

Miha and Nick had become great friends, so Nick bluntly asked Miha, "Can I bring someone else to talk to you?" The screen then flashed with many faces as it did before. Then the screen went dark. A second later, Nick saw a word in the middle of the screen, and it was in the most beautiful colors he had ever seen. The word read

"YES"

Chapter 8: Nick

It took Nick many weeks to recover since his friends
entered the Higgs Field. It was a whirlwind of
activity, and he needed time to absorb what had just
happened. He was, after all, just human, and he was a
broken person because he had just lost two of his
closest friends, but he knew more than most about the
Afterlife, and his recovery came somewhat fast. After
all, he knew where his friends went and hoped he
would go there too.

He needed to get his thoughts together on how to
proceed. Although he already knew the nurse that he
would introduce to Miha, he wanted to meet with her
one more time. Her name was Jennifer, and he had
known her since he was hospitalized in Denver with
complications from his paraplegic condition.

The nursing staff at this Denver hospital was the heart
& Soul of the hospital, just like it is at every hospital
in the country, but Jen, as he called her, was the best
of the best. She wanted to work up to the senior level
of CNIO (Chief Nurse Information Officer) and was
studying computer science as it relates to the medical
profession. She already had all the other factors for
the job and was looking for a job opportunity. The
true humanity in her was exceptional. She was real,
and he knew it.

Jen started her nursing career in Rapid City, South
Dakota, where she met her life-long partner (Chris).

They were both new to their careers back in the mid-late 1970s.

Jen was compassionate towards all patients, but two twin American Indian kids tugged on her heart more than most. She helped these two grow up during her last two years in Rapid City because their parents had been killed in a horrific drunk driver accident. The kids were twins, but one female and one male. The female was named Maka Red Elk, and the male kid was Chaiton Red Elk, and they did eventually live with their aunt in North Rapid, but Jen spent a lot of time with them during these two years and helped them get back on their feet again. They both became like her own children, and it was very difficult for her to move to Denver when she was offered a significant raise, but she kept in close contact with both Maka and Chaiton through their grade school years and into Junior High. It was in Junior High that she started to lose contact, and it seemed to Jen that they were both trying to find themselves, so she just stayed available in case they called, but of course, she always sent birthday cards and other holiday cards. Jen even learned some of the Lakota language to be closer to them.

Chris knew Maka Red Elk and Chaiton Red Elk through Jen. Chris didn't have the emotional and human skills to feel like Jen towards these two kids, but he learned a lot about Lakota ways and had deep respect for the American Indian people.

One evening was especially significant. In the late

1970s, Chris was called to a stabbing just north of a new Safeway store on East-North Street. When he arrived, he found two kids, both stabbed by one another, and one was Chaiton. He immediately called for two ambulances, and both kids were taken to the hospital. Jen was on duty that night and learned of Chaiton's wounds, so she called in help as needed. Unfortunately, the other boy was less fortunate and passed away on the way to the hospital.

Chaiton's stabbing wounds were not life-threatening, and he fully recovered.

Later that week, Chris was driving off-duty up East-North Street when he noticed a small circle of American Indian people around the very spot where the other boy had been stabbed. Chris stopped his truck and walked over to the circle but stayed in the back out of respect for the family. One of the older men saw Chris and welcomed him into the circle, and they stayed for about a half hour. At one point, Chris looked up and saw Chaiton in the distance, and he knew that Chaiton was going to have a hard time with this, even though it was found that Chaiton was defending himself. It would leave a deep emotional scar on Chaiton because the other boy was really his friend, so Chaiton was also glad to see Chris helping the family of the boy that died. His name was Mato.

Jen felt for Mato and his family and helped as she could, but the family didn't know Jen and was not as accepting of her help. It was a horrible incident, and they never found a reason for the knife fight. What none of them knew at the time was that Mato jumped to the Higgs Field.

Current time and back in Denver......

That's how Jen was; she loved people, and caring for people was one of her callings. For this reason, Nick called her and made arrangements for lunch the next day.

Jen was excited to see Nick again and in such good condition, but she was a little surprised about why he wanted to meet.

Nick told Jen he had come across a wonderful medical device that she might be interested in due to technical, medical advances. He said it was created by one of his good friends and was not patented yet, but it showed promise, and he wanted her opinion.

Jen was a little shocked, but she trusted Nick fully because they had many late-night talks about death and the Afterlife.   Jen helped Nick through a very serious surgery that he was not expected to make it through, but Nick did make it and made a full recovery, or at least as much as he could, being a paraplegic from before the surgery.

It was a great reunion between Nick and Jen, and at the end of lunch, Nick had no reservations about bringing Jen into this wonderful discovery. Nick invited Jen for what would be the adventure of her lifetime.

The next Saturday, Nick picked up Jen in his modified muscle car. Nick drove a 1971 Chevrolet Camaro, which was perfect, including the modifications he made to drive it in his paraplegic condition. Nick fully controlled this vehicle and showed Jen what 1970's engineered muscle cars could do. She loved it and was impressed by how Nick had full control.

After nearly getting stopped by the police (twice), Nick settled his driving down, and they arrived at the location of the Afterlife Machine (AM, as he sometimes called it).

Jen was a little apprehensive but followed Nick into the room where the computer and cooling device was set up. She was surprised and impressed by the setup, even though it was messy, with fast-food wrappers and empty soda and beer cans all around the room.

Nick asked Jen to sit beside him and right in front of the two video screens. Then Nick turned on the mechanism, and things came to life.

Nick didn't know it, but Miha was kind of a jokester. Miha manifested himself as a hummingbird flying in the middle of the screen. Nick then said, "where are you, Miha." Then, the hummingbird started to talk with his tiny beak and slowly transformed into the image of Miha that Nick was most familiar with.

This sight was so stunning of a transformation that Jen just started to laugh. She laughed uncontrollably for a full minute, with Miha and Nick watching on in confusion. When Jen was finished, her mouth dropped in shock and amazement. She asked Nick, "what's going on, really? I mean, what's going on?". That was Nick's clue to get the explanation going.

Nick asked Jen if she wanted to talk with someone she knew that had recently passed. A strange look came across Jen's face, but she didn't flinch. She had just lost a patient to what is called Amniotic Fluid Embolism. This is a condition during birth when amniotic fluid enters the mother's bloodstream and causes massive blood loss and other reactions that are not fully understood. It is the worst type of traumatic birth, and she was heartbroken when the doctors could not revive this first-time mother-to-be named Sara.

When Jen was a new nurse temporarily stationed at the Kaiser Hospital in Santa Clara, California, she saw a patient that also experienced Amniotic Fluid Embolism. It is a rare occurrence, and many medical professionals do not come across it within their careers, so the fact that Jen saw this twice was unusual. The occurrence when Jen was younger was shocking, to say the least, but the doctors were able to save the 35-year-old mother named Lyn, and the baby, too, was okay because he was born just before the reaction occurred. His name was Ashe. Jen also remembers this case because the husband of Lyn

(Mac) was in the room when all hell broke loose. Jen has a vivid memory because this was her first Code Blue experience. Doctors and nurses came running into the room from all directions, and one of the lead Doctors quickly took charge of finding the bleeding. Although Lyn had lost most of her blood, the Doctors and Nurses were quickly supplementing blood and blood products. This effort kept Lyn alive, and while this was happening, Jen was the one that had to tell Mac that he needed to leave the room immediately, but he only went to the hallway, holding his new baby in shock and disbelief. He would not leave his wife, and in fact, he would eventually stay by her side until she recovered. The look on his face at that time has never left her memory after all these years. Lyn did have months to recover. This young family was able to continue their lives together, and that was heartwarming to the entire hospital staff.

Unfortunately, the situation was much different for Sara. Although Sara was in great shape, the bleeding was too fast for the medical team to replace her blood, and the hospital was not as well equipped. Her heart stopped, and after five tries to recover Sara, she was gone. Sara's husband and family were devastated. It's hard to think of her husband continuing without his wife and the baby without a mother, let alone the grandparents and other family members. It was a horrible situation, and it continues to weigh terribly on Jen. Not many medical professionals have seen this situation because it is so rare, but it does, unfortunately, occur, even in these modern times. As a result of this situation, Jen knew exactly who she would like to talk to from the other side of life.

Jen, with suspicion, said to Nick why do you ask such an unreasonable question, and Nick quickly answered that he had a way to communicate with those that passed.

Over the next several hours, Nick explained the story of Bret, Barb, and Miha. All the way through the explanation, Jen had her hands to her mouth in shock. It was kind of funny to Nick, but he continued to the end, and through all of this time, Miha simply watched Jen's expressions.

Then it was time to make introductions.

"Jen," Nick said, "I'd like to introduce you to Miha. Miha is our connection to the Afterlife."

Jen looked at Miha, and Miha looked back at Jen from the computer screen. Jen said nothing. She was in shock at the situation for several minutes. Then Miha said, "do you know why animals die?". Jen slowly mouthed…. "No ." Then Miha said, "To get to the other side ." It took a couple of seconds, and then Miha and Nick broke out laughing, and Jen started to smile too.

This broke the ice, and Jen started to talk directly to Miha rather than through Nick. Jen was starting to trust this unimaginable situation.

By the afternoon, Jen was well informed of the past, and she was a believer. "Wow, how incredible," she said. Then she turned to Nick and said point blank. "Why are you showing me this?".

Nick stuttered a little but finally said he needed her help. He had just lost his best friends and was unsure of things. Nick said that he knew she had been through hell with COVID deaths within the hospital and that she might be able to get some relief from this mechanism and also help him on how to proceed with it. That's when Jen stood up and yelled, "You Betcha," and Nick immediately said, "What do you mean? Jen apologized and then explained that these were the first unusual words that came to her mouth; she explained that she was from the Midwest. She said she would be honored to be with Nick on this adventure.

Chapter 9: THE NEXT STEP

After introductions and this extraordinary meeting, Nick drove Jen back to her house. Jen explained that she needed time to fully understand what had just happened and to also plan out a path forward.

Jen was a single lady working towards her retirement years. She wasn't married, but as previously mentioned, she dated a man named Chris Taylor. Chris was an experienced Investigator with the city and county of Denver, Colorado. Although she didn't live with Chris, they usually spent the nights at one or the other's homes. She loved Chris, and Chris loved her, but they just weren't married. It was the best relationship that they could come up with, given they both had difficult jobs with horrible hours. Having children was never an option, but they both saw each other as life partners to retire with and live out their lives together.

Chris was a veteran Investigator. He had been with the Denver Police Department for 20 years including being an Investigator for the past 10 of those years. As mentioned earlier, he worked in Rapid City, South Dakota, as a young police officer.

Chris was originally from Rapid City, just like Jen, and made many trips back there every year. He loved to fish Rapid Creek and spend time in the livelier parts of the downtown area with Jen, but he also loved living in Denver. It was just a bigger Rapid

City, but the fishing wasn't near as convenient. In fact, nothing was, except it had more sunshine in the winter, and he loved the winter more than any other season. Unfortunately, he didn't have much time for fishing or sitting in the sun these past years. Denver was experiencing an increase in crime, and overtime pay was plentiful. Chris's life was mainly work and spending time with Jen, and this was fine with him. He would do anything for Jen, and going out with Jen was how he de-fragged his mind and relaxed.

The life of Jen and Chris stayed mostly the same, except for hours, they always changed due to job requirements, but Jen started to feel a need to visit Nick and the wonderful mechanism that he had. How could she not? This was a way to see past physical life itself, and she had so many that she wanted to contact, both from work and from personal life. What a gift it was to have this available, but she was sworn to secrecy about it and could never tell Chris.

Chris was in no way a jealous person, he never was, but he was an Investigator by profession, and something was just not right. The next few months became more concerning with time. He didn't want to check up on Jen, it made him feel like a loser, and he wanted her to have freedom without explanation. Unfortunately, the Investigator in him started to check into things.

Jen, in the meantime, was spending more time with Nick and the mechanism. She spent the first days talking with Sara about how she felt and how the situation unfolded. Sara was naturally interested in her husband and baby while in the Higgs Field. The Higgs Field didn't offer the insight that she had while with the Whole-One.

Nick wasn't ready for Jen's request, but he fully understood, and they started planning in order to bring in Sara's husband and young child, now about a year old. It took much preparation. Jen and Nick needed to make contact with Sara's husband in a soft and easy way. After all, how do you tell a widowed husband that he can see and talk to his wife, that passed a year ago?

Chapter 10: START OF INVESTIGATION

It took a few months, but Chris was now worried. He loved Jen, and he would fight for her if need be. So privately, he started to look into Jen's timelines and explanations, and he realized that she was seeing a person named Nick.

Chris had a lot of investigative tools available to him, but he needed to make sure that whatever he did make sense. He couldn't simply do a background check on Nick, even though that's exactly what he wanted to do.

With stealth, Chris learned that Nick was a paraplegic. He then wondered what kind of relationship they might be having. Chris had a wonderful relationship with Jen, and he thought that he satisfied Jen in every way, even though he knew he was kind of a tough guy. Chris reasoned things out in his mind and then was able to get back to work….and sleep.

On one beautiful sunny winter day, Chris decided to take a mental health day. The office was busy as usual, but less happened in the previous days, so he took the day off. Jen went to work as usual, and Chris made his favorite eggs with Colorado green chili sauce. As he sat down with his breakfast, he heard the name Nick multiple times on the local TV. It seemed that this was the same Nick that knew Jen, so he listened intently.

Several people had second and third-hand information about a miracle device that allowed talking with those that died. This news started as a quack and a joke, but over time others came forward talking as if this wasn't some kind of conspiracy theory. Conspiracy theory or not, Chris knew he needed to learn more in order to make sure Jen was safe.

Weeks passed, but every so often, this same subject came up in the Denver news, and it became a joke on the Denver radio stations. Nobody really paid much attention to it, but this subject was just coming up too much.

Chris finally decided to meet with Nick during off hours. Chris showed up un-invited to Nick's place one evening and introduced himself as an investigative reporter who has worked for the Denver police many times. Nick was a little startled by this and thought this was just another ploy to get more information about the crazy machine that some others were telling the Denver media.

Nick wanted this issue to go away, so he wheeled out on the front patio in order to talk with this reporter named Chris. Nick did not want the person inside his house at all and was going to try to stop the reports if he could. Nick explained that the people spreading these rumors were people that he did try to help with grief. Nick said that he thought he helped them by showing others online with similar issues, but that was all. He simply wanted to help them with other articles and pre-recorded videos of others that had also lost loved ones. Nick said he was very surprised that these people told a different story, and he was sorry for the misunderstanding.

During this informal meeting, Chris, as an experienced Investigator, could tell that something was definitely odd. Now Chris needed to look into this situation regardless of his relationship with Jen. This situation was just weird.

At work, Chris finally decided to open up an investigation into Nick. It was more of an investigation into what so many others in Denver had said about some kind of miracle device. Denver police didn't know what miracle the device performed. Information was so convoluted, coming from second, third, and sometimes fourth sources.

Typically, an Investigator would have chalked this up to locals wanting to get on TV or to just second-hand PLUS information, but Chris continued with reverence. He loved Jen and had known her well for many years. This was not just some nutty news article.

Chapter 11: FAMILY REUNION

Sara's widowed husband was named John, and this past year was hell for him. A couple of John's siblings helped a lot, but they both lived long distances away, and John's parents were never any help because they had one of those horrible marriages in which they argued amongst themselves most of the time, sometimes physically, so John always felt sorry for them, and their marital problems, and never asked them for help, even while growing up. Fortunately, it was Sara's family that helped him survive with his new infant, and Sara's sister Jessica was the most help. She cared for baby Harry, and she loved him deeply. Jessica was Sara's younger sister by two years and took on many of Sara's features, but the best thing about Jessica was her natural skill with infants and young children.

The hardest times were the first few months. Baby Harry needed a lot of attention, and John was constantly confused and tired. Sara's parents arranged a schedule for someone to stay at John's house at all times in order to help with the baby and, of course, the funeral. It was all a blur to John, even a month after Sara's funeral.

Sara's brother-in-law helped John with the insurance claims and money issues, and fortunately, John had good insurance and a well-paying job. Within the second month, John was able to go back to work, with Sara's sister babysitting during the days. John would come home at night and take care of the baby through the night until he needed to go back to work the next day. It was very hard, but the baby made life worth living.

As the year stretched, month after month, life became more normal, and John's emotional breakdowns became less and less. John was learning to live life again.

The call from Nick came out of the blue for John. At first, he thought it was another sales call for car insurance and almost hung up, but that's when Nick said he had some excellent news about Sara. Of course, John was interested, and a lunch meeting was set up at one of John's favorite places called Angie's in Littleton, Colorado. It was quiet and comfortable. This lunch took place during the work week, so John had a normal lunch period before he needed to be back to work.

The conversation started with introductions, and then Nick told of his past friends and the mechanism that was built. John's interest was full-on intense during the entire conversation. John was fully engaged at each stage of the conversation, and Nick told him the long version. John's interest remained until his cell phone rang. It was Sara's sister, Jessica, asking why John hadn't come home. The time was now 6:00 PM. This conversation was so intense that nobody realized the time except the restaurant, of course. Nick paid the bill with a well-deserved tip, and they both went to the parking lot.

A time was set up for Saturday, when Jen, John, and baby Harry would go to Nick's house, where he had the AM ready, with Miha standing by.

The next Saturday came up quickly, and everything was ready. Jen sat close to John, who sat down with baby Harry in his lap when Miha introduced himself. Although John thought he had prepared himself for this, he started to shake a little. Then the screen widened, and he saw Sara, the love of his life, next to Miha. John lost it on the spot but gained control after a minute. Then John and Sara had a long conversation about that horrible night, but finally, Sara told John not to worry anymore. Sara explained to John that the Higgs Field and being with the Whole-One was unimaginable joy and happiness. She explained that she would be waiting for the time for John joins her and that she would grab his hand and run off with him in total elation, and that's when it happened.

As Jen and Nick sat there listening, they all heard a noise from baby Harry. When they looked down at him, he was looking straight at Sara. Then he said as clearly as can be, "Mama." Jen lost it and ran out of the room in tears. Nick teared up as well, and John hugged Harry with gentle love. Even Miha turned his head so that no one could see that he still had some emotion in the Higgs Field. This was truly a special moment, and Sara was astonished by joy. You see, Harry still remembered Sara's voice from when he was within Sara, before being born.

When everyone regained composure, Miha had some special news, which Sara already knew. Miha explained that the Whole-One doesn't put forth more than a person can endure, and what happened with Sara was one of those situations that pushed the limit. In these situations, some unusual help is provided by the Whole-One, and that is why Sara's family was available to help John this first year, and Jessica was literally a Godsend. John and Jessica were becoming closer, and Sara knew this was absolutely wonderful.

It was great to see the odd reunion, but it was also disheartening to see the physical separation. These visits did occur, though, and all involved did get some form of satisfaction and solitude.

The situation of seeing one's loved ones on a computer screen and at the same time being physically separated had one main issue, and that was loneliness in the 3D+T for the physical survivors. The pros were so much larger, though, and it became apparent that they were doing the right thing. It was for this reason that Jen and Nick spent more time together without even thinking of Chris.

Chapter 12: MIRICLE MEETINGS GIVING HOPE

Even though some information was leaking out to the news about the AM (Afterlife Machine), Jen and Nick continued with the emotional help of those that lost loved ones, particularly to COVID. Jen and Nick didn't really think these leaks would amount to anything, and for this reason, they continued to briefly and sparingly offer the AM to those that they vetted. Vetting for Jen and Nick meant to find those that were in deep mourning with unusual circumstances and would be willing to keep the secret of the AM. This was difficult to do, and they knew that word would get out. However, they moved the AM every so often out of Nick's place in case an inquisitive reporter would nose around.

Chapter 13: THE INVESTIGATION

Learning of the investigation from Chris into Nick caused an immediate reaction from Jen. Although Jen was a reasonable person, like Chris and Nick, she lost it. It might have been the stress of trying to get deceased loved ones in contact with those that still lived, or just the raw emotion that was needed by each. In either case, Jen lost it and started to yell and hit Chris.

Chris was surprised but sympathetic. He knew Jen, and this was extremely unusual.

The next morning, they talked. Jen reluctantly lied and made up a story about Nick on the spot because she could not reveal the real Afterlife Machine. She talked about how Nick thought he was helping people that recently lost loved ones. She was purposely vague about the details. As a result, she made up a story that Nick thought he could communicate with the dead and that Jen was trying to help Nick understand that this wasn't possible, so she attended all of Nick's "medium" meetings. She told Chris how she knew Nick and that Nick was not a threat to either one of them. Chris did not believe any of it except how they met in the hospital years ago, but he listened to everything that Jen said. What he heard sounded like some kind of conspiracy theory, and he believed that Jen was caught up in it.

Chris's feelings for Jen didn't change, though, and he was going to save her from this situation that Nick created. He would investigate Nick further, but without Jen knowing.

Chris was an excellent investigator and knew something was odd, and he knew she wasn't telling him everything, but his experience told him that she was in danger. Jen was an excellent nurse and was exceptionally compassionate. She needed to keep this secret from Chris, at least for now. The fact that they were both great at their jobs was literally causing them personal issues. Neither one would want to lose the loving relationship that they had, but the situation was causing them to separate emotionally, at least a little.

Jen knew her explanation was weak at best, but it was all she could do on-the-fly. She needed to come clean with Chris, but she needed to talk with Nick first. After all, Nick talked to her in confidence about the AM. Jen would bring this up with Nick at the next meeting.

In the meantime, Chris started to think of getting a warrant to search Nick's home. He didn't know what he would find, but he felt that what Jen said about Nick was not correct. Nick didn't even talk about being a medium when they met originally, and the Denver news never mentioned a medium, either.

The next morning Chris got up extremely early and went to the office in order to start paperwork on the search. This gave Jen a chance to schedule a time to meet with Nick about getting Chris into the loop of

this miracle machine. She relished in the thought of Chris becoming involved with her and Nick.
Due to busy schedules, she agreed to meet with Nick on Saturday, several days in advance, as it was only Tuesday.

Chris finished his paperwork late Tuesday and started planning his team members. The more he thought about it, the angrier he got. In fact, he decided he would make up a story to Jen that he had a tight deadline on an important undercover case and that he would not see her for several days. He slept in his office at night but spent most of his wake time researching Nick and the Denver news articles, as well as why Jen would lie to him. She had never lied to him before; why now? It just didn't make any sense.

On Wednesday, Chris talked to his supervisor (Joe) and laid out his strategy for searching for Nick's home. He had his team picked out and only needed his supervisor's okay, as well as the warrant, of course.

Joe was surprised by what Chris was planning because it was not like Chris to plan for a search for such a minor issue. For this reason, he told Chris to get back to him on Thursday or Friday in order to better explain the case and reasoning for the search. Chris knew he was getting ahead of himself, and understood Jim's concern, so he left the meeting determined to have solid reasoning by Friday. This gave him two days to make a solid case for the search, and he would start with surveillance of Nick.

Chris parked his car near Nick's home but out of view. The evening started and continued slowly. Nothing much happened. It was unlike Chris, but he fell asleep while watching Nick's home, but nothing happened Thursday night anyway, so Chris drove towards the office at about 10:00 AM. That's when he saw Jen's car traveling towards Nick's place. Chris turned around and re-parked out of sight, watched Jen walk up to the door, and was let in. About an hour later, Jen left Nick's. "What the Hell," Chris thought to himself. He then decided to tell Jim everything that he saw and hoped that he would agree to the warrant request.

What Chris didn't know was that Nick and Jen found time to talk about getting Chris informed of the Afterlife Machine, and Nick was in full agreement. Nick was a little worried about Chris, and this just felt right to bring him on board. Jen was as happy as could be with this news and couldn't wait to tell Chris. She called Chris while she was leaving, but Chris didn't answer. He was burning with anger.

Jen made many calls to Chris on Friday in order to give him the good news, but Chris refused to answer. Chris was hell-bent on the warrant to search Nick's property, and Chris did get the Okay from Jim. A warrant was requested, and it was signed by a Judge. The search would happen first thing on Saturday, so Chris slept in the office Friday night.

Jen became worried about Chris, but she knew undercover operations were difficult, so she just waited it out, but she had a pre-arranged meeting with Nick for Saturday morning anyway, so she thought she would just bring breakfast to Nick as a surprise.

Saturday morning started with a beautiful sunny day, typical of the Front Range of Colorado, but this morning was different.

Jen stopped at Santiago's restaurant in order to get four breakfast burritos, two for Nick and two for her; although she couldn't eat two, she felt like celebrating.

Jen pulled up at Nick's house just as Chris and the Denver Police were initiating the search warrant. It was a tense time for the Denver Police because any search warrant was scrutinized for every detail, and they wanted perfection, but perfection was not what happened. The Denver Police were caught off-guard when Jen pulled up holding a paper sack that looked to contain long objects.

Chris was nearby watching this unfold from his supervisor's position and was horrified to see the reaction of the Denver Police. They told Jen to "STOP" and "DROP THE WEAPON." Just then, Nick opened the door, and this caused more confusion and anxiety among the Police.

Jen didn't really know what was happening, but she had been with Chris's buddies many times and was comfortable walking towards them, but with the confusion of a potential weapon, and Nick at the door, the Police took defensive positions. Unfortunately, one rooky was spooked enough he shot off two rounds at Jen as she stepped forward.

Chris, watching from his position, yelled, "STOP, PUT YOUR GUN DOWN!" But the damage was done. Jen hit the driveway hard, with her head pounding off the concrete twice.

Jen jumped to the Higgs Field before her head hit the second time. One of the bullets pierced her heart dead-on. Jen died that fast.

The next actions are still somewhat confusing, as Nick came out the door in his wheelchair, bouncing off the steps, and Chris also came flying from his position towards Jen.

Denver police detained Nick easily, but Chris wasn't going to have it. He literally slammed his fist into the rookie's face and then dropped next to Jen in panic. Several of his officers tried to contain Chris, but he was enraged and eventually put two of them in the hospital before about four officers restrained him.

With both Nick and Chris down and restrained, the scene was secured, and the warrant was obviously canceled.

Chapter 14: FUNERAL

Eleven Days later, the funeral for Jen was scheduled. During these days, a full investigation of this horrible day was conducted, and no charges were made against the rookie that shot Jen. He was found correct to reasonably think that the paper sack contained a weapon, given that Jen was not stopping. That the elongated objects in that sack were burritos was an extremely unfortunate truth but could have resembled a gun barrel.

Chris was also cleared of any wrongdoing. The rooky that Chris hit and the other two officers that he put in the hospital were released in good order; nobody pressed charges. Even if they did, no jury would have convicted Chris. He was a shell of himself after this day and didn't react too much. Mostly he just stared in the distance, but he did get good care from his department and was told to take two weeks off or more if needed. A Psychologist was also paid to visit Chris every other day through the first week of Chris's absence, and this helped Chris regain some composure.

During this same time, Nick was in shock. The scene happened so fast and out of the blue; it just seemed like a nightmare. Everything was going so well up until Saturday. The death of Jen compounded Nick's depression over the death of his best friends, Bret and Barb. Too many deaths in such a short period. How could this have happened? Jen spoke so well of Chris, and yet it was Chris that planned this whole ordeal. Nick went into a deep depression, but he would attend the funeral, of course.

Jen's funeral was on a Tuesday, and the weather was perfect, as it is most of the time in Colorado. Jen would be buried on a day just like her personality, sunny. Nick noticed this, but Chris did not. Nick, knowing of the Afterlife, had a much better understanding of the Soul, but Chris did not, even though Chris was a believer in God. It was during this funeral that Nick's anger for Chris evaporated, and by the end of the ceremony, Nick wanted to fulfill Jen's wishes of bringing Chris into the loop of the AM. After all, what a gift it would be for Chris to understand that physical life is just one part of the Soul, but he needed to be careful because Chris was not himself, and Nick didn't know what to expect.

The funeral was beautiful. Many of the Denver Police and Police officers from surrounding suburbs attended, particularly after learning of this tragic event, in order to show support for Chris. Also, both Jen and Chris were somewhat known in the metro for the work they had volunteered for and the number of years that they worked in Colorado, but it wasn't just Denver and Metro Suburb Police that showed up. Two members of the Rapid City Police Department also attended. They remembered Chris, but they also knew Jen extremely well. They were Maka Red Elk and Chaiton Red Elk, and they came out of deep respect for Jen and to offer support to Chris. Chris nearly fell over when he saw them both, and they sat up in front with Chris. Chris didn't know that they were part of the Rapid City Police Department and couldn't be happier for their success. They wore traditional American Indian headdresses, with Rapid City Police shirts and pants. They were a wonderful sight for Chris.

The church was big and had two levels for attendees. Each police department had different colors, and they all sat in order and together. From high up in the stadium, you could see that at least 20 agencies were represented in different colors, and it was an impressive sight. Outside, two Fire Department Ladder trucks crossed the extended ladders with a large American flag hanging in between.

Both the Denver Police and Rapid City Police Departments had speakers because they all knew Jen. It was just a beautiful service, but at one point, Chris needed to get up and stretch, so he walked to a nearby isle and looked up at the fully packed stadium seating. He locked eyes with Nick. What was Nick doing here, he thought, but it was natural that Nick would be here given the time they spent together. Chris just didn't know the details. Although Chris was determined to find those details out, he didn't know that Nick was just as enthusiastic about letting Chris know those details.

And then, the service was over, and life needed to go on for everyone. Nick asked Maka and Chaiton Red Elk to come back in a couple of months in order to stay with him for a few days, and they agreed, although they didn't like the busyness of Denver much. Just too many people for them; nothing personal about the people. More open spaces were in their blood.

Chapter 15: AFTER THE FUNERAL

After the funeral, Chris went back to his condo. It was a two-bedroom in a high-rise on the 27th floor with a beautiful city view. The building was on the outskirts of the taller buildings in Denver's LoDo (lower downtown) neighborhood. He owned the place, just as Jen owned her condo on the 14th floor of this same building, except Jen had an unobstructed mountain view beyond Denver's western suburbs. They both had legal paperwork such that in case of death, the other one would inherit all properties and savings. As a result, Jen's condo was now his, and he needed to go through both places, but it was too hard to go to Jen's condo just yet. He was having a hard time going through her stuff at his condo.

Picture by author, Denver, Colorado, July 5, 2022

Chris eventually kept the things that mattered and offered her other material things to the homeless that he encountered, and they saw the value and grabbed it up fast. This was okay with him because that's exactly how Jen would have wanted it. He would eventually do the same with Jen's things within her condo, but he took emotional breaks in between, and it took a few months, but it was good. He now had his place as usual, and Jen's place with typical furniture only, like a bed in each of two rooms, kitchen appliances, couch, tv, etc., and he could sell the place as-is very quickly because it was move-in ready.

But before he sold it, he was sent a text message from Nick. It was cryptic at best. It read: "Please, I want to let you in on a secret that Jen wanted for you, something about the Afterlife of those that have passed."

Chris didn't understand Nick, and the reason for Jen's visits with him, so this might be an opportunity for him to find out more of the truth, and that's exactly what Nick wanted. Nick wasn't any threat to Chris, so why wouldn't Chris respond?

Before responding, Chris wanted to sleep on this. He always slept on difficult issues if he could, and in this situation, he felt he could take his time.

That night Chris had a dream. It was Jen, and he reached out to her, but to his surprise, he saw two hands reaching out to him, one was Jen, and the other was of an elderly American Indian. Chris shifted in sleep and briefly woke up, and then re-entered the same dream with Jen approaching. Chris reached out his hand again, and once again, he had two hands reaching out to him; one was Jen, and the other was of an elderly American Indian, but this time the American Indian wore the headdress of an Indian Chief. The headdress was worn and bloodied but was mainly intact. This woke Chris up immediately, and he got up for the day, making coffee, and getting ready for work, two hours early.

During the next day, Chris couldn't get that dream out of his mind, and eventually, he started to think of Maka Red Elk and Chaiton Red Elk, and then he thought about the young kid Mato, that was killed in the knife fight with Chaiton.

The next day Chris felt the need to visit Maka and Chaiton Red Elk in person, so he just got in his car and headed north on I-25 toward South Dakota. Somewhere around Wheatland, Wyoming, he called his boss and told him that he wasn't going to make it into the office that day because he had something important to do. His boss asked for more information, but Chris didn't offer any. Chris's boss knew that something was off but didn't want to ask more questions, so he simply told Chris to take care and to let him know if he could help in any way. Chris's boss was a good man and knew enough to give his employees some leeway when needed, and this was certainly one of those times.

Chris had taken many routes between Denver and Rapid City, including going through Scotts Bluff, Nebraska, and also the route through Torrington, Wyoming, but this time he traveled up I-25 to highway 20 and took a right near Orin, Wyoming, towards Lusk, Wyoming. Chris loved to go through Lusk, Wyoming, because it was such a clean little town. Chris had spent some time there over the last 40 years and learned about the best motels and to also eat at Lira's restaurant just south of town. Chris loved Lira's and ate there every time he had the chance, but this time he needed to get to Rapid City as soon as possible, so he just passed through Lusk and headed up towards Edgemont, South Dakota.

As Chris traveled north, he was just a few miles from the turn-off at Mule Creek Junction, and he suddenly felt faint. Chris nearly passed out at one point but recovered quickly. He turned right onto highway 18 towards the Wyoming-South Dakota border and Edgemont, South Dakota, about 10 miles further. Chris enjoyed this part of the trip as the highway entered the Black Hills in such an unpopulated area. It was always nice to get out of Denver and up to God's Country.

Chris went through Hot Springs, South Dakota, and then onto a winding highway to highway 79 that would take him into Rapid. It was midafternoon, and Chris was feeling good driving in this beautiful country, but suddenly near the intersection that went to Buffalo Gap, South Dakota, he felt faint again, so he pulled over. While there, Chris looked over at the ridge separating the Black Hills from the prairie and saw three American Indian people in full Indian attire from the 1880s. One is on a beautiful white horse, and he has his arm extended out towards Chris, with his fingers spread apart as if waving support. Chris reluctantly brought his hand up in similar support, and just like that, the three American Indians and Horses vanished.

What, what just happened? Chris thought. Was I hallucinating? Chris sat there on the lonely road for a few minutes and then reminded himself that he had just one more hour on the road before checking in to the Alex Johnson hotel in downtown Rapid City, and then he could relax. When in Rapid. Chris calls Maka Red Elk and Chaiton Red Elk in order to buy them dinner and beers at the Firehouse restaurant in downtown Rapid. Chris wants them with him for contact with Nick. Even though Chris is a tough guy, he's uneasy about this spooky situation Nick has and thinks that his Lakota friends might be of some help.

Chris tells Maka Red Elk and Chaiton Red Elk that they can stay at Jen's place, which has a couch, TV, and two beds. He said he would buy new bedding too. Then Chris went back to Denver while his friends decided when to visit Denver. Two days later, Maka Red Elk responded that they would attend, but no bedding was needed; just let them know when to arrive, and that's when he decided to accept Nick's offer, but only if he could bring Maka Red Elk, and Chaiton Red Elk with him.

Nick accepted the terms and trusted Chris. After all, Jen trusted Chris, and Nick was out of options. Nick was exhausted by the deaths of his friends and the extreme situations. They arrange to meet at Nick's place at 10:00 am the next Tuesday.

On the Monday before, Maka and Chaiton arrive at Jen's place and settle in with the key that Chris previously sent them. Chris met Maka and Chaiton at Jen's and was surprised to also meet an American Indian Elder called Takota. Takota looked at Chris and said, "Do you remember me?". Chris said, "I'm sorry, but I don't." Takota explained that he was the person that welcomed Chris into the circle during the funeral of his son back in the late 1970s. Chris immediately remembered, and they talked about that difficult time. This conversation helped Takota and Chris to communicate in a reminiscing way, and they got along great. Takota was older, of course, but they now had more in common, and Takota felt that he could trust Chris more than before.

Takota went on to explain a little more about the stabbing. He explained that Mato was a good boy but had a temper when it came to his girlfriend. Chaiton had helped this girl earlier with a school issue. It seemed that some other girls were making fun of her, and Chaiton stepped in to defend the cruel rumors. That was it, but Mato thought that Chaiton was moving in on his girl, so he challenged Chaiton to a fight. It was a horrible misunderstanding, and this helped Chris feel better about Chaiton. Up to this point, Chris always had some suspicion about Chaiton in the back of his mind. Now he knows with no uncertainty that Chaiton was innocent that night. This set the record straight.

Chris and his three visitors pulled up at Nick's house at 9:50 am, a little early, but Nick was ready for them. Nick invited them into the house and offered food and drinks, but nobody wanted anything, so Nick took them downstairs toward the Afterlife Machine (AM).

While standing in the downstairs hallway, they made polite introductions, and Nick showed where the kitchen and the bathroom are in case anyone needed something, but again, no one wanted anything. Nick told everyone but Chris to go into his office down the hall. Then Nick told Chris that he needed a few moments with him. Nick explained to Chris that he was very sorry for the death of Jen and that Jen wanted to bring Chris on board with the secret that he was about to witness. This conversation only took a few minutes, and then they both walked to Nick's office. As he walked towards the office, he could hear Takota, Maka, and Chaiton talking loudly in the Lakota language. When he arrived, he saw that they were talking directly toward the two computer screens and that they were talking to another American Indian person.

Chris sat down and listened, but he didn't know very much of the Lakota language.

It seemed that the person on the computer screen was a close friend of Crazy Horse, and he was talking fast in Lakota, and it was something about Paha Sapa or the Black Hills.

Then Takota turned to Chris and asked if he had ever heard of an Indian by the name of Hotah. Chris did remember a story told of a small Band of Lakota Indians that outsmarted the United States Army back in the 1880s, and Takota said that was right. Takota went on to say in English that Hotah had the same situation as they do now in regard to ownership of the Black Hills. Takota explained that Hotah could not attack friendly white settlers in order to maintain his hunting grounds and that modern Indian people could not expect existing white settlers to simply give up their property to the age-old contract between the US government and the Indian people.

Then the conversation went back into the Lakota language, but Chris could make out words that were not in a Lakota language, such as State Lands and Federal Lands.

To Chris, it sounded like a strategy for how to solve the age-old land agreements between the Indians of the Black Hills and the United States Government.

But that's when Chris heard a loud voice, not from his area or from the computer screen. It came from, well, everywhere and nowhere. It was at that point that the American Indian person on the computer screen (the close friend of Crazy Horse) slowly faded from the computer screen, and Takota, Maka, and Chaiton simply got up and walked out of the room. That left only Nick and Chris in front of the computer screen, and Nick moved to the other room, but within sight of Chris.

Chris was confused. Why did everything change all of a sudden? Then out of the corner of his eye, he saw Jen on the computer screen

Up to this point, Chris didn't know what the AM was or any history of the Afterlife Machine. He was shocked and motionless, and then he started to think this was some kind of trick and stood up in a huff. Nick was not far off and was nervous at this reaction, but then Jen said in a loud voice, "Sit Down!" Chris had only heard Jen say this a few times, but he knew it was Jen, and only Jen could have made him sit down, so he did. Then Jen told Chris in a more sympathetic voice, "Chris, I know this is bizarre, but please, you need to listen to what Nick has to say, and it is critical that you learn the truth. I'll talk to you once you learn the truth to this miracle machine". Then she was gone from the screen.

Chris then looked at Nick, and Nick looked back. Nick then said, "hey guys" (referring to Takota, Maka, and Chaiton), "now is a good time for you to come back into the office" Takota, Maka, and Chaiton did come back, and they all sat in a circle to talk about what just happened.

Nick started by talking directly to Chris, "Chris, what you saw is really Jen, but her Soul is with God now. She is in an interim place in which we can communicate, and this is the secret that Jen wanted to share with you". It was simpler for Nick to talk in these direct ways to Chris, at least in the beginning, and that's when Nick told the long story of his experiences.

Now that Chris was up to speed on this AM, Chris wanted to reconnect with Jen as soon as possible, but he wanted more of a private meeting with just Jen, him, and maybe Nick. For this reason, Chris asked everyone to leave the room. After they left, Chris spent several hours talking with Jen about the horrible event that he had planned. Chris realized that his anger had gotten the best of him, and he lost his life partner, at least within the 3D+T.

When his emotional conversation ended with Jen, Chris had a million questions, but for some reason, he asked who it was that was talking to Takota, Maka, and Chaiton and how did they accept this communication so fast while he and Nick had a short conversation in the hallway? Nick didn't really have an answer, but he suggested that the Lakota have a better understanding of life and the past life. That's when Takota spoke. He said that it was not surprising at all to learn that past relatives exist in a different place, but that he was surprised to talk through technology, like the computer screen. Takota explained that the person they were talking to was actually a friend of Crazy Horse and that past experience with another great warrior may be needed in order to help solve the impasse that exists between the United States of America and the Indian people of the Black Hills. Takota went on to say that this conflict needed to be solved in order for the white settlers and the Indian people to become one society because they are stronger together than apart. He said that a past warrior by the name of Hotah solved a similar but much smaller conflict and that Hotah solved it in a humane and non-conflicting way. Then Takota thanked Nick for the insight, and this part of the conversation ended.

Chris, as well as Takota, Maka, and Chaiton, were all intensely interested in the Afterlife machine, particularly after seeing it for themselves, so Nick explained everything. Although the Lakota have true belief in the afterlife, the story of this Afterlife Mechanism, the super cold environment, and the quantum Higgs Particle/ Field were all new information and interesting as hell. Takota finally said that science is starting to catch up with realism, and he warned Nick to stop the use of this Afterlife Machine until more can be learned about the consequences. He then told Nick that he would like to speak to some others back in the Black Hills about this. He gave his word that he would not talk about specifics but rather that he would talk in generalities as to what the Indian Elders would do if they could have direct contact with those that passed rather than through dreams.

Everyone in the room was silent for at least two minutes. Two minutes may not sound like a lot of time, but it is when you're in a meeting with many others.

The next one to speak was Nick. He liked the idea of pausing the effort to offer this AM to others. The leaks to the Denver news were not good, and they (Nick and Jen) may have been moving too fast. Another minute of silence went by, and then Maka spoke. She agreed with the pause and suggested that all of them agree to the fact that they have somehow become connected in an extremely important group, whether they liked it or not, and she said that from now on and in the future that they were more than brothers and sisters. They were now in possession of a life-changing machine. The implications were enormous.

It was from this day on forward that the Team was established. The first members had perished in the creation and early implementation of the machine, but now they were going to control this wonderful device.

The full list of Members of this new club is as follows:
- Bret Zimberman in Higgs Field/Whole-One
- Barb Zimberman in Higgs Field/Whole-One
- Nick
- Jen in Higgs Field/Whole-One
- Chris
- Takota
- Maka
- Chaiton
- And, of course, Miha, from his many lives.

This meant that five members lived in the 3D+T or the 4-Space environment. It meant that out of the billions of animals that existed on planet earth, only five people had access to the incredible machine that Bret Zimberman stumbled across in his somewhat convoluted logical thoughts of a zero-temperature environment.

This was a huge responsibility for them all, and they all realized the impact of any wrong decision. They were now committed together like a family. Given the implications, they all committed to absolute secrecy and to help each and every member out when any issue arose.

Chapter 16: WARRANT MOVES FORWARD WITHOUT CHRIS

The following week, Chris went back to the office full-time. Everyone was sympathetic, and Chris didn't want that at all. Chris wanted some normality like the office was before Jen's death, but he knew that his co-workers would need time as well in order to start treating him normally again.

Chris picked up his previous workload and started to catch up. He was behind in several cases because he had put everything on hold for the search warrant for Nick's property.

It seemed strange now that he was in full support of Nick and the newly formed team. It was just a few weeks ago he felt so much anger toward Nick. He had made bad assumptions in the past and thought he had a better handle on knowing what to do, but this mistake would affect him for the rest of his physical life.

A week went by, and it was Monday again, and Chris was settling back into work again. People were still treating him differently, so it was of no concern to him that his Boss (Jim) wanted to meet with him at 9:00 am. Chris thought it was for moral support, but he was wrong.

When Chris entered Jim's office, it was full of other co-workers. Chris sat down, and Jim started the meeting off. Jim told Chris that while he was away, he personally began the process of requesting another warrant on Nick's home. Jim told Chris that he and others were bound and determined to seek justice for Chris and Jen.

Shocked was an understatement, but Chris had a good poker face. They didn't know that Chris was friends with Nick, and he couldn't explain the changes that took place without talking about the AM. It was for this reason that he pretended to go along with this sting operation.

What was a surprise was that the warrant was going to take place at noon today. Chris immediately thought to himself, how was he going to tip off Nick and maintain his stealth in doing so? Chris needed to think quickly because he knew he would have little to no time by himself between this meeting and noon, and he couldn't use his cell phone because they would trace any calls from his phone.

Fortunately, he was part of a close nit team now, and he could call on one of the other team members for help, but at the same time, he didn't want any ties to them either.

The entire investigative team was in motion now, and vehicles were being packed up and readied for a fast trip to Nick's house. While this was happening, Chris asked for attention, and everyone stopped, including his boss, Jim. Chris explained that he appreciated the work everyone had done and the support he had been given, and it was at this time that Jim started to clap his hands and said to Chris that they would always support those on team blue (meaning the police). Then Chris thanked everyone one more time and emphasized that they should be careful on the warrant and show some care in handling Nick's things because he is still not found guilty of anything. That's all Chris had to say, but when he looked at Jim, he received a strange look as to why Chris had just said what he did. Then the preparations continued.

Chris decided to call Chaiton and ask him to warn Nick from a public phone or another phone that would not directly tie the call to Chaiton. Chaiton understood and made the call to Nick from a phone he borrowed from a hotel clerk at the Alex Johnston Motel in downtown Rapid City. The call was brief, and Chaiton whispered to Nick that a warrant had been issued and that the Denver Police would be there by noon or before.

Nick, in his paraplegic condition, could not move as fast as he wanted to, so he decided to simply disconnect the cooling device from the computer and take it to a hiding place somewhere…, but where? If he drove, he would not be sure that he wasn't followed because the house might be under surveillance now. The fact that this cooling device came from Russia didn't help at all, and in fact, it could lead to a much broader form of investigation.

At the time Nick was trying to figure out how to hide the cooling device, three black SUVs and one dark blue sedan traveled fast toward Nick's place.

It was 5 minutes to 12:00 noon when all vehicles pulled up, and most everyone rushed to the door in order to serve the warrant on Nick, and Chris was right there in the back of the pack.

Nick answered the door and was handed the warrant. Then everyone entered and spread out. Nick and Chris looked at each other briefly, and Nick seemed relaxed. This made Chris a little less nervous, and he observed the rest of the police team take things apart, especially the computer. A cardboard box was next to the computer, and Jim looked under it. Nothing was there, except wires that went to the computer, but were not connected, so he asked Nick what was in the box. Nick said he had a speaker there, but it didn't work out.

Chris noticed a group of police standing in the doorway to the garage, so he walked over. One of the policemen said, "This Nick character rocks; look at that Camaro." They walked in, and some were already inside the garage looking around while another policeman opened the hood. The engine was impressive and had some equipment that the police would not recognize because it was modifications to the steering, breaking, and accelerator due to his paraplegic condition. Another policeman said that this looked complicated, and Chris agreed because of the modification for Nick to drive. That's when Chris looked at the components better. "Holy Shit," Chris thought as he noticed something bolted to the frame. Chris noticed the cooling device bolted to the internal frame with some fake wires as if it was part of the modifications. Chris thought to himself, "what a perfect disguise," and after seeing this, Chris was glad to have Nick on his side. After all, who could have thought of this, and how did he do it so quickly, Chris wondered.

Then one of the police investigators said, "Shit, Look Up, Everyone." Everyone then looked up and saw a network of rails, pullies, and controls on chains that were hanging from the ceiling. Also, there was a body wrap that would fit around Nick. One policeman said, "this Nick not only ROCKs, but he's also a smart guy. Look how he created the means for him to work on the engine himself."

Another policeman said that he was going to take pictures and patent this device, but he didn't know that Nick had already done that. The only thing remaining was how to stabilize his body when turning tools. Hanging on the chains made him torque when he turned wrenches.

After two hours, the police had wrapped up the computer and some paperwork, but nothing else looked suspicious. The police didn't take anything off the car, so the cooling device was never realized.

That was a close one, Chris thought. They wouldn't be able to use the AM for a while, but they were taking a break from it anyway.

The computer and other things that the police removed from Nick's home were all returned about a week later. Nothing was broken.

Chapter 17: A TIME TO REORGANIZE and PLAN

The AM Team consisted of five people within the 4-Space environment. They kept in regular (monthly) contact with only two telephone numbers; one was Chris's cell phone for Chris and Nick, and the other was a landline used jointly by Takota, Maka, and Chaiton in Rapid City. The monthly call after the warrant on Nick's place was a long conversation. Clearly, they knew Nick was under the microscope, and that needed to change.

The Team decided to keep Jen's place and use it for the AM in the future, with everyone having access. All team members pitched in some money monthly in order to pay their share.

They decided that when they took someone to visit the AM that they would take them to Chris's place first, on the 27th floor, and they would make sure that the person knew that they were on the 27th floor, but without seeing Chris. Then they would put opaque glasses on them so they can't see and take them up and down on the elevator a few times. Then they would turn them around so they didn't know they were on the 14th floor (Jen's floor). At this point, they would take them into Jen's old condo on the 14th floor, but the person would think they were on the 27th floor (Chris's place).

Photo by author, Denver, Colorado, 7.5.2022

This was done for obvious reasons, to give them the impression that they were on the 27th floor and in Chris's room. If the person then told the media, they would be directed to a Denver Investigator's home, and Chris could easily squash any rumor of the AM.

This overall plan was starting to take shape, and the team members also started to accept the awesome responsibilities of being team members. Things were looking up for them all. They all had difficult lives, and this might have been the plan. The Whole-One would not want the privileged to take on this tasking because the Whole-One needed real people that experienced real life with all of the struggles of normal life.

During the next few months, Chris and Nick would visit Takota, Maka, and Chaiton in Rapid City, and Takota, Maka, and Chaiton would travel to Denver too. They were starting to get along together and learn about each other's life struggles. They even talked about traveling together in order to just see other parts of the country. They were truly becoming a family.

Several months passed, and Jen's death faded a little. Chris was living again, and thanks to his new team members, he felt alive again. Of course, he knew of the Afterlife, and this made a living in the 3D+T world easier. He wanted to see Jen more, but Miha told him that he must learn to live in the 4-space environment without her. The AM was not a substitute for them both to depend on. Jen, of course, knew this, but Chris wanted the security of seeing her, but that is not how it works.

Takota, Maka, and Chaiton also wanted to use the AM to contact many past tribal members, and this was okay at first, but Miha had to also explain to them that the AM was not to be used as a substitute for regularly conversing with those that passed. The Whole-One was giving a short period of conversation in order to show the continuance of the Soul to a select few people beyond the 3D+T. That was all, and the Team was taking things beyond the intent of the Whole-One.

It didn't take long for the Team to get the message, and they all talked about it. It was then that they all realized that they were given an incredible and special gift, but now they knew the limits, and they would keep those limits.

The next day was a wonderful revelation for them because they all experienced the same dream the night before. The dream was that they needed to get the word out about the Cycle-of-the-Sole, and this AM (Afterlife Machine) was a tool to be used sparingly to do that. The team could use the machine as proof of the Higgs Field, and the Whole-One. The Whole-One knew that modern physics had advanced to the quantum level, and that the quantum weirdness proved of at least one other dimension beyond the 4-Space or 3D+T. Virtual particles move back and forth to this dimension by the trillions every micro-second, and that's only within one person's body. The Whole-One knew that modern physics would soon discover smaller building blocks of matter than quantum particles, to include where positive and negative "Charge" came from. This was a pivotal period of time where humanity was about to find out about the Cycle-of-the-Sole. Modern physics was now being integrated with absolute proof of the Whole-One.

For the Team, it felt like life just began for them all and that a weight was lifted from them. The pressure of using this machine for continuous purposes was causing extreme stress, and they didn't even realize it, but now they did, and it was relaxing. They would now use the AM to prove to Psychologists, Nurses, Religious Leaders, Heads of States, and others to show proof. They were all together during this revelation, and happiness broke out with them all.

Nick was as happy as he could be at this moment, and that's when the Whole-One called for him to come home again, and Nick wanted this with the whole of his being.

Nick went to the Whole-One in a flash. Within the 3D+T world, he had a heart attack, but in reality, he had fulfilled his ultimate tasking for the Whole-One. He had helped in initiating the Team that would solidify proof that the Sole exists, and the Sole can become one with the Whole-One.

Nick jumped to the Higgs Field so fast he didn't know what was going on. At first, he was with his four best friends in the 3D+T, and the next thing he realized was that two sets of hands were reaching out to him. They were from Bret and Barb Zimberman, and Nick was thrilled to be with them again, but they weren't the only ones. So many others were there that he could not see all of them surrounding him from all sides. All those within the Higgs Field knew of this accomplishment, and were in harmonic joy to see successful contact with an outstanding group of people in the 3D+T. This was going to change everyone's conception of what physical death was and how it integrated with the Cycle-of-the-Sole.

Nick was so thrilled he didn't even realize that he wasn't in a wheelchair anymore. He felt so natural.

Nick turned to look at his friends on the other side of the computer screens and waved to them, just like when Bret and Barb waved at him after their passing.

The four remaining members of this special Team were in total shock but in complete joy to see Nick out of his wheelchair and being welcomed by so many. It was incredibly sad to see him go, but it felt right that Nick made it to the Higgs Field. Nick was with the Whole-One once again, but this time it was different. Nick would not return to the 3D+T ever again. Nick was now **Brahman**.

END

References
(In the order shown in this book)

- Life Afterlife, by Raymond A. Moody Jr.,
  M.D., published 1975 by MBB, Inc., and later
  published by Bantom Books, 1976, copyright
  1975, 2001, 2015.

- Closer to The Light, by Melvin Morse, M.D.,
  published by Random House Publishing
  Group, Copyright 1990.

- SPECIAL REFERENCE: BASIC SUPER
  FLUIDS, by Tony Guénault, CRC Press, Taylor
  and Francis Group, Boca Raton, London, New
  York, 600 Broken Sound Parkway, NW, Suite 300,
  Boca Raton, Florida 33487-2742.

- SPECIAL REFERENCE: THE
  STRANGEST MAN, The Hidden Life of Paul
  Dirac, Mystic *of the* Atom, by Graham
  Farmelo, Copyright 2009, hardcover first
  published in the United States in 2009 by
  Basic Books, A member of the Perseus Books
  Group. Published in Britain in 2009 by Faber
  and Faber Limited, Paperback first published
  in the United States in 2011 by Basic Books.
  Basic Books, 250 West 57th Street, 15th Floor,
  New York, NY 10107.

- The Island in the Plains, A Black Hills Natural History, by Edward Raventon, 1994, Johnson Printing Company, 1880 South 57th Court, Boulder, Colorado, 80301

Definitions

Brahman – (From Wikipedia, the free encyclopedia, 2021):   In Hinduism, *Brahman* (<u>Sanskrit</u>: ब्रह्म) connotes the highest universal principle, the <u>ultimate reality</u> in the <u>universe</u>. In major schools of <u>Hindu philosophy</u>, it is the material, efficient, formal and final <u>cause</u> of all that exists. It is the pervasive, infinite, eternal truth, consciousness and bliss which does not change, yet is the cause of all changes. *Brahman* as <u>metaphysical</u> concept refers to the single binding unity behind diversity in all that exists in the universe.
Brahman is a <u>Vedic Sanskrit</u> word, and it is conceptualized in Hinduism, states <u>Paul Deussen</u>, as the "creative principle which lies realized in the whole world". *Brahman* is a key concept found in the <u>Vedas</u>, and it is extensively discussed in the early <u>Upanishads</u>. The Vedas conceptualize *Brahman* as the Cosmic Principle. In the Upanishads, it has been variously described as <u>*Sat-cit-ānanda*</u> (truth-consciousness-bliss) and as the unchanging, permanent, highest reality.

Brahman is discussed in Hindu texts with the concept of Atman (Sanskrit: आत्मन्),
(Self), personal, impersonal or *Para Brahman*, or in various combinations of these qualities depending on the philosophical school. In dualistic schools of Hinduism such as the theistic Dvaita Vedanta, Brahman is different from Atman (Self) in each being. In non-dual schools such as the Advaita Vedanta, *Brahman* is identical to the Atman, is everywhere and inside each living being, and there is connected spiritual oneness in all existence.

Causality - (From Wikipedia, the free encyclopedia, 2021): Is the relationship between causes and effects. While causality is also a topic studied from the perspectives of philosophy, from the perspective of physics, it is operationalized so that causes of an event must be in the past light cone of the event and ultimately reducible to fundamental interactions. Similarly, a cause cannot have an effect outside its future light cone.

Copenhagen Interpretation: (From Wikipedia, the free encyclopedia, 2021): The Copenhagen interpretation is a collection of views about the meaning of quantum mechanics principally attributed to Niels Bohr and Werner Heisenberg. It is one of the oldest of numerous proposed interpretations of quantum mechanics, as features of it date to the development of quantum mechanics during 1925–1927, and it remains one of the most commonly taught. There is no definitive historical statement of what *the* Copenhagen interpretation is. There are some fundamental agreements and disagreements between the views of Bohr and Heisenberg. For example, Heisenberg emphasized a sharp "cut" between the observer (or the instrument) and the system being observed, while Bohr offered an interpretation that is independent of a subjective observer or measurement or collapse, which relies on an "irreversible" or effectively irreversible process, which could take place within the quantum system.

Features common to Copenhagen-type interpretations include the idea that quantum mechanics is intrinsically indeterministic, with probabilities calculated using the Born rule, and the principle of complementarity, which states that objects have certain pairs of complementary properties which cannot all be observed or measured simultaneously. Moreover, the act of "observing" or "measuring" an object is irreversible, no truth can be attributed to an object except according to the results of its measurement. Copenhagen-type interpretations hold that quantum descriptions are objective, in that they are independent of physicists' mental arbitrariness.

Over the years, there have been many objections to aspects of Copenhagen-type interpretations, including the discontinuous and stochastic nature of the "observation" or "measurement" process, the apparent subjectivity of requiring an observer, the difficulty of defining what might count as a measuring device, and the seeming reliance upon classical physics in describing such devices.

Der Stürmer (From Wikipedia, the free encyclopedia, 2021) (pronounced [deːɐ̯ ˈʃtʏʁmɐ], literally "The Stormer / Attacker / Striker") was a weekly German tabloid-format newspaper published from 1923 to the end of the Second World War by Julius Streicher, the Gauleiter of Franconia, with brief suspensions in publication due to legal difficulties. It was a significant part of Nazi propaganda, and was virulently antisemitic. The paper was not an official publication of the Nazi Party, but was published privately by Streicher. For this reason, the paper did not display the Nazi Party swastika in its logo.The paper was a very lucrative business for Streicher, and made him a multi-millionaire. The newspaper originated at Nuremberg during Adolf Hitler's attempt to establish power and control. The first copy of Der Stürmer was published on 20 April 1923. Der Stürmer's circulation grew over time, eventually distributing to a large percentage of the German population, as well as Argentina, Brazil, Canada, and the United States. The newspaper reached a peak circulation of 486,000 in 1937.

Unlike the <u>Völkischer</u>
<u>Beobachter</u> (The <u>Völkisch</u> Observer), the official
Nazi Party paper, which gave itself an outwardly
serious appearance, Der Stürmer often ran obscene
material such as the <u>blood libel</u> and
graphic <u>caricatures</u> of Jews, as well as sexually
explicit, <u>anti-Catholic</u>, <u>anti-communist</u>, and anti-
<u>monarchist</u> propaganda. As early as 1933, Streicher
was calling for the extermination of the Jews in Der
Stürmer. During the war, Streicher regularly
authorized articles demanding the annihilation and
extermination of the <u>Jewish race</u>. After the war,
Streicher was convicted of being an accessory
for <u>crimes against humanity</u>, and was executed by
hanging.

Determinism (for physics only) - (From Wikipedia, the free encyclopedia, 2021): Cause and Effect. Since the beginning of the 20th century, <u>quantum mechanics</u>—the physics of the extremely small—has revealed previously concealed aspects of <u>events</u>. Before that, <u>Newtonian physics</u>—the physics of everyday life—dominated. Taken in isolation (rather than as an <u>approximation</u> to quantum mechanics), Newtonian physics depicts a universe in which objects move in perfectly determined ways. At the scale where humans exist and interact with the universe, Newtonian mechanics remain useful, and make relatively accurate predictions (e.g. calculating the trajectory of a bullet), but whereas in theory, <u>absolute knowledge</u> of the forces accelerating a bullet would produce an absolutely accurate prediction of its path, modern quantum mechanics casts reasonable doubt on this main thesis of determinism.

Entropy - On-Line Dictionary: A thermodynamic quantity representing the unavailability of a system's thermal energy for conversion into mechanical work, often interpreted as the degree of disorder or randomness in the system. "the second law of thermodynamics says that entropy always increases with time" · "the sum of the entropies of all the bodies taking part in the process"

Entropy - (From Wikipedia, the free encyclopedia, 2021):s a scientific concept as well as a measurable physical property that is most commonly associated with a state of disorder, randomness, or uncertainty. The term and the concept are used in diverse fields, from classical thermodynamics, where it was first recognized, to the microscopic description of nature in statistical physics, and to the principles of information theory. It has found far-ranging applications in chemistry and physics, in biological systems and their relation to life, in cosmology, economics, sociology, weather science, climate change, and information systems including the transmission of information in telecommunication. The thermodynamic concept was referred to by Scottish scientist and engineer Macquorn Rankine in 1850 with the names *thermodynamic function* and *heat-potential*. In 1865, German physicist Rudolf Clausius, one of the leading founders of the field of thermodynamics, defined it as the quotient of an infinitesimal amount of heat to the instantaneous temperature. He initially described it as *transformation-content*, in German *Verwandlungsinhalt*, and later coined the term *entropy* from a Greek word for *transformation*. Referring to microscopic constitution and structure, in 1862, Clausius interpreted the concept as meaning disgregation.

A consequence of entropy is that certain processes are irreversible or impossible, aside from the requirement of not violating the conservation of energy, the latter being expressed in the first law of thermodynamics. Entropy is central to the second law of thermodynamics, which states that the entropy of isolated systems left to spontaneous evolution cannot decrease with time, as they always arrive at a state of thermodynamic equilibrium, where the entropy is highest. Austrian physicist Ludwig Boltzmann explained entropy as the measure of the number of possible microscopic arrangements or states of individual atoms and molecules of a system that comply with the macroscopic condition of the system. He thereby introduced the concept of statistical disorder and probability distributions into a new field of thermodynamics, called statistical mechanics, and found the link between the microscopic interactions, which fluctuate about an average configuration, to the macroscopically observable behavior, in form of a simple logarithmic law, with a proportionality constant, the Boltzmann constant, that has become one of the defining universal constants for the modern International System of Units (SI).

In 1948, <u>Bell Labs</u> scientist <u>Claude Shannon</u> developed similar statistical concepts of measuring microscopic uncertainty and multiplicity to the problem of random losses of information in telecommunication signals. Upon <u>John von Neumann</u>'s suggestion, Shannon named this entity of *missing information* in analogous manner to its use in statistical mechanics as *entropy*, and gave birth to the field of <u>information theory</u>. This description has been identified as a universal definition of the concept of entropy.[4]

Kelvin – (From Wikipedia, the free encyclopedia, 2021): The kelvin is the base unit of temperature in the International System of Units (SI), having the unit symbol K. It is named after the Belfast-born Glasgow University engineer and physicist William Thomson, 1st Baron Kelvin (1824–1907).

The kelvin is now defined by fixing the numerical value of the Boltzmann constant k to 1.380649×10^{-23} J·K^{-1}. Hence, one kelvin is equal to a change in the thermodynamic temperature T that results in a change of thermal energy kT by 1.380649×10^{-23} J.[1]

The Kelvin scale fulfills Thomson's requirements as an absolute thermodynamic temperature scale. It uses absolute zero as its null point (i.e. low **entropy**). The relation between kelvin and Celsius scales is $T_K = t_{°C} + 273.15$. On the Kelvin scale, pure water freezes at 273.15 K, and it boils at 373.15 K in 1 atm.

Unlike the degree Fahrenheit and degree Celsius, the kelvin is not referred to or written as a degree. The kelvin is the primary unit of temperature measurement for the physical sciences, but is often used in conjunction with the degree Celsius, which has the same magnitude.

ALSO relating to Kelvin (From Wikipedia, the free encyclopedia, 2021) – Absolute Zero: Absolute zero is the lowest limit of the thermodynamic temperature scale, a state at which the enthalpy and entropy of a cooled ideal gas reach their minimum value, taken as zero kelvins. The fundamental particles of nature have minimum vibrational motion, retaining only quantum mechanical, zero-point energy-induced particle motion. en.wikipedia.org

Metaphysical – (From Wikipedia, the free encyclopedia, 2021): Metaphysics is the branch of philosophy that studies the first principles of being, identity and change, space and time, causality, necessity and possibility. It includes questions about the nature of **c**onsciousne**ss** and the relationship between mind and matter. The word "metaphysics" comes from two Greek words that, together, literally mean "after or behind or among [the study of] the natural". It has been suggested that the term might have been coined by a first century CE editor who assembled various small selections of Aristotle's works into the treatise we now know by the name *Metaphysics* (μετὰ τὰ φυσικά, *meta ta physika*, lit. 'after the *Physics* ', another of Aristotle's works).

Physics - (From Wikipedia, the free encyclopedia, 2021): Physics (from Ancient Greek: φυσική (ἐπιστήμη), romanized: physikḗ (epistḗmē), lit. 'knowledge of nature', from φύσις phýsis 'nature') is the natural science that studies matter, its motion and behavior through space and time, and the related entities of energy and force. Physics is one of the most fundamental scientific disciplines, and its main goal is to understand how the universe behaves.

www.ingramcontent.com/pod-product-compliance
Lightning Source LLC
Chambersburg PA
CBHW020240130626
46549CB00005B/1986